Beyond Telling

Beyond Telling

stories

Jewel Mogan

Ontario Review Press / Princeton

"Age of Reason," "Mad," "X and O"
originally appeared in *Ontario Review;*
"The Proselyte," in *Mademoiselle;*
"See Ya Later, Floydada," in *Thema.*
"Age of Reason" was reprinted
in *The Pushcart Prize, XIX.*

Cover photo by Jewel Mogan

Library of Congress Cataloging-in-Publication Data
Mogan, Jewel.
Beyond telling / Jewel Mogan.
Contents: Age of reason — Mad — The proselyte —
Wade in the water — Syzygy — Desaparachos — A certain lot
or parcel of land — X and O — Doucet's last paradox —
See to appreciate — See ya later, Floydada — Beyond telling.
1. Louisiana—Social life and customs—Fiction.
2. Texas—Social life and customs—Fiction.
I. Title.
PS3563.033B49   1995   813'.54—dc20   94-39166
ISBN 0-86538-082-1 (acid free)

ONTARIO REVIEW PRESS
Distributed by George Braziller, Inc.
60 Madison Ave., New York, NY 10010

A pity beyond all telling
Is hid in the heart of love . . .
          —W. B. Yeats

CONTENTS

Beyond Telling

Age of Reason

Nana read to them under her bed lamp as she always did when their grandaddy, whom they called Grundy, was working late at the market. She read for Rachel something from her photo-copied church materials that she felt was suitable for eleven-year-olds, while Tolliver made gentle flopping movements with his limbs, occasionally throwing his leg over Nana, putting his fingers into her ears and his, taking the fingers out, lacing his fingers together, crooning to himself sleepily. He sensed when the moral of the piece had been hammered out and said, "Now. My turn."

"Not yet. Shh."

He shushed. He was exceedingly well-mannered for a four-year-old. Their grandmother finished reading the material—it had to do with the gifts of the Spirit—and Tolliver reached over to the bedside table for his book, *Jesus Loves Me*. Rachel, nestling closer to her Nana, listened to this story too, although she had heard it a hundred times. She decided she would read the words backwards. She liked to do this when they were riding around. She liked to be Alice in Backwards Land and read billboards and signs backwards. She and her brother rode around a lot with Grundy and Nana. When Grundy was one with the Spirit they rode all kinds of places, him talking fast and loud, there and back, and Nana lots of times not saying a single word, which their grandaddy never noticed. When he was that way they visited church friends and prayer groups one behind the other, attended every revival for miles around. She often wondered what they would pick up and do next. On the good side, they went to Putt-Putt or the Dairy Queen when they were not doing church things. Once, on a day that was a dream come true, they drove to Dollywood! They were in paradise for an unforgettable eight hours.

At one of their picnics to Standing Stone State Park, Grundy had been inspired and had run around shouting, "I understand every thing! I understand every thing!" And something about the universe, the universe. He shouted many other holy things, like "Two men will be out in the field; one will be taken and one will be left. Two women will be grinding meal; one will be taken and one will be left." And "Ha. Ha. Safe are the blessed in the bosom of the Lord!" and he and Nana sang. He kind of shook Nana into singing, shouting, "Good God, woman, don't anything move you? I am moved by every thing!" After they ate lunch, Nana got him to calm down by them praying in tongues until he was slain in the Spirit and it turned into a short nap. Rachel and Tolliver wanted permission to go and look at the waterfall. They waited, watching his jerky movements as he slept. When he was waking up, Rachel (she knew to do this) had crept up to him softly on her knees and spoken to him gently. He had screamed.

They were always changing. They changed houses. Once they just moved down the street. They changed cars, but only one rattletrap for another, changed telephone numbers most of all, changed friends within their church. Her grandaddy had never changed occupations; he had always been a butcher. But he had worked at all the supermarkets in Cumberland County, there not being more than half a dozen big grocery stores in these mountains. He rearranged the furniture, the contents of the garage, and the car trunk over and over. He carried butchering tools around in the trunk—an extra cleaver and big knives. Recently she had watched him add a hatchet and a long-handled ax to the cleaver and knives. He wasn't happy at the market where he was now, but he had told Nana he just as well stay there for the two years until his retirement or the Rapture, whichever came first. The Rapture had just been invented at that time, and their whole church was beginning to buzz about it.

They never changed churches. They all spent endless hours in Jesus's one house while games went unplayed, races unrun. They could have been taking giant steps or petting puppies. Not their own puppies—they had no pets—but Whatzit, the Neilsons-next-door's dog, had puppies. Five wriggling, cuddly, adorable little puppies. She would give anything to have any one of them, especially the one with two white feet. She could sit and watch him and pet him by the hour.

In church there was body twisting and clapping, love-shouts and singing, nasal, trembly, same-note singing. Tolliver slept through even the noisiest parts of it, stretched out on the wooden pew, but Rachel would alternately doze and jolt awake until it felt like she was sitting on pins and needles and she wanted to scream. Her legs were so jerky they wanted to run for miles and her body wanted to throw itself down in lush grass and roll around. When they had the chance, how feverishly they played on the Neilsons' lawn before darkness descended. She thought she would like Sheila Neilson's church, First United Methodist. It sounded kind and strong. But, no, they never changed churches. She hoped that when they were taken up, God's heaven would be more interesting than His house.

She had been able to attend the same school in spite of all their changing: the beloved big-little school whose library she had squeezed dry from Aladdin to Oz, starting with the animal books. All the books were perfect. There were only grades of perfect and superperfect. *The Little House on the Prairie* by Laura Ingalls Wilder, for example, as dear as it was, couldn't compare with *Caddie Woodlawn* by Carol Ryrie Brink. The magic names of the authors, often repeated reverently to herself, were part of the unshakableness of the titles. She, too, would have three names when she grew up. Several times a year she checked out *Caddie Woodlawn* just to see if it was still as good, and it almost always was. She sometimes checked it out and back in on the expiration date unread. It was important just to have it near her, on her bed, or the table or chair next to the bed. She always brought Caddie along on their trips.

Caddie slipped away to join Tom and Warren on the back step. They sat together, and Nero lay close to their feet. Out by the barn, Robert Ireton was strumming his banjo and singing softly. Something something something. Then *Behind the barn there were northern lights, long white fingers shooting up in the blackness of the sky; and the three adventurers were overcome by that delicious weariness which suddenly overtakes one at the end of an outdoor day.*

"Em sevol suseJ," she murmured, as Nana read *Jesus Loves Me* and Tolliver put his hands palm to palm, prayerlike. She watched, fascinated, as he placed thumb to forefinger on each hand and made graceful movements with them, like his hands were two deaf people talking to each other. Jesus loves Em. She called herself that sometimes. Backwards me.

She looked up from the pillow to Nana's sweet saggy face. There was a small permanent indentation in Nana's lower lip where in cold weather she tore at the tiny tatters of skin with her teeth or sometimes with her fingertips, repeatedly peeling off skin. Rachel watched the depression in her lip move as her lips moved. Nana never changed anything about herself. She wore the same two or three outfits all the time. She sighed a lot over the world and people's troubles. When her voice would trail off without finishing its sentence, you had to finish it for her, but usually, you knew what she meant to say. You couldn't rush Nana. When you did, she would always say, "I can't think. . . . I can't think. . . ." When Grundy frowned, Nana frowned. When he laughed, she smiled.

Rachel hungrily kissed her grandma six times on the side of

her face. She was getting drowsy, so she said goodnight and went to bed before *Jesus Loves Me* was over.

Between the short simple sentences of the book the grandmother could hear the schoolhouse regulator on the opposite wall limping. She had told Ernest, her husband, that it was limping. It was going tock-TICK tock-TICK all night long, she had told him. He told her, "If it's out of beat, it's not enough for me to hear." Later, he said, "I adjusted it very slightly." She could hear it now, going tock-TICK tock-TICK again. She guessed it was out of beat just enough to distract her, but not enough to cause it to stop beating.

Tolliver was still signing to himself as she read. When she finished his story he wandered into salad talk, gradually diminishing to a whispered conversation with himself. The whispers floated up to the bed lamp and he watched them with fixed, luminous eyes. Suddenly he was asleep. She switched off the lamp and was already lonesome for him. There would be a few precious minutes before Ernest came home. In the dark she lifted Tolliver's hand, so yielding it frightened her, took her breath away. She kissed his fingers, brooded, prayed fervently with his fingers to her moving lips. She put him to bed in his own small room. Then she went back to her bed and lay still, gave herself over to silent crying which she stifled immediately Ernest came in.

He was not one in the Spirit at this time, so they greeted each other as she expected, solemnly and shortly. He took off his pants and shirt, which always smelled of blood, balled them up with his underwear, threw it all into the clothes basket. When he was not in the Spirit he would not shower. A shower would not make him clean, he said. When he was in the Spirit he showered twice a day and he seemed to want sex nearly every day. Tonight he put on his pajamas and rolled solidly into her flank and into sleep. She took up crying again. It was three years since the children's mother, their daughter, died, and their father deserted the family.

She couldn't see the face of the clock on the opposite wall. It was that dark in the bedroom. Ernest liked it pitch black. She wouldn't be surprised, even if she had light, if that clock wouldn't turn its face away from her on purpose so she couldn't see the time. TOCK-tick. TOCK-tick. The times were turning out so bad. The time for the Rapture had come and gone. It had been a bitter disappointment to her and Ernest and a large segment of their church that nothing had happened. She prayed now over the new date that had been set, not for the Rapture, but for the End. It was coming very soon, the day after Easter. Would it be by fire, this time? Oh, then the clocks would throw their hands to their faces in terror.

It was hours until she slept.

But now everything was fresh and young.
"A magic time of year," Caddie called it to herself. She loved both spring and fall. At the turning of the year things seemed to stir in her, that were lost sight of in the commonplace stretches of winter and summer.

The long long Palm Sunday service was over. Tolliver was still in his Wal-Mart suit and tie—Midget Man, Rachel called him on Sundays when he was dressed like this—and she was in her new navy blue long cotton dress with a high ruffled neck, long sleeves with ruffles at the end, white stockings, and black patent leather shoes. Her hair was in two pigtails with bows on the ends to match her dress. Nana was wearing her gray and white long-sleeve meeting dress and white patent leather bag that was turning yellow where she held it.

They were driving out into the country; Grundy said it was a surprise where they were going. He had on a brand-new suit of a pinkish-brown color and a purple tie. Maybe it was the tie that made the suit look pink. He was in the best mood she had ever seen him. He sang swingy gospel songs and when he couldn't think of any more songs, he sang made-up ones: "Safe are the blessed in the bosom of the Lord" and "Jib jibber-jibber jab, and jab jabber-jabber jib!" And laughed, Ha-ha! Tolliver laughed his head off with him. She heard that silly rhyme and Tolliver's piping laughter all that night after they got home and went to bed.

They had left the main highway with its gray limestone outcroppings on either side that seeped water all the year round, but more so in the spring. The country road they were on was leading back into green hills. It was so beautiful out the car windows. Cornfields were shooting up all over and every so often they would glimpse a white farmhouse, tall and narrow, tucked back in the fold of two hills as they rounded a bend in the road. Between two other hills she saw the spider web of a tiny train trestle and a dark green river underneath. Then suddenly, they were turning in at one of those narrow farmhouses.

"Dunk knows you are coming for the lamb?" Nana asked worriedly.

"It's waiting for me. He's selling off half of his lambs next week. I got in on a good thing. He's giving me wholesale slaughter price on it."

"A lamb?" Rachel asked. "Are we going to get a lamb?"

"For our Easter dinner," said Nana.

It was a little boy lamb, and he was the most precious thing Rachel had ever seen or imagined in her most tumultuous rush of maternal love for the Neilsons' puppies, or Whatzit, or her baby dolls. His eyes! And his white woolly body, delicate little legs, and tiny hooves. You could still pick him up! although Dunk said he was as grown as he could be and still be called a lamb. His little cries! He was unbelievable. On her knees, Rachel hugged him and stroked his thick yielding wool and gently dug her fingers into it. She longed to take him home for her own and care for him. All that she would do for him went through her mind in vivid flashes. She pictured his bed in a wooden box of straw in the corner of the garage next to the warm water heater, and the milk, and other as-yet-undetermined things she would feed him—she wasn't sure what lambs ate—and the purple and pink ribbons she would put around his neck.... And violet-colored

bows! She would put violet bows on his precious woolly ear-
flops. Neither she nor Tolliver had ever had a pet. Tolliver
hugged him hungrily, too, said Ahhhh, put his head down on the
lamb's neck and nuzzled the wool. They couldn't stop admiring
all that whiteness and those melting eyes, his panting sides, his
flanks.

But they weren't going to take him home. Not alive, anyway.
Grundy had parked around the back of the barn and Dunk
pointed out a spot for him to do the slaughtering that had a
wooden table and a faucet and trough. Grundy got his white coat
and tools out of the trunk. After he got the coat on, he took off his
pants from underneath the coat. He took off his shoes and socks
also.

No one watched, not even the farmer. Dunk's wife gave
Tolliver and Rachel some lemonade and they sat on the back
steps of the house with their heads drooping. They could hear
Grundy behind the barn praying out loud over the animal with
his gift of tongues, spinning webs of words, hanks, strings of loud
words from the Bible and his own mind, while the lamb bleated
every now and then. Rachel imagined that the cries must be very
strong back there, but weakened by the time they reached the
steps where she and Tolliver sat. Then there weren't any more
sounds. Her heart was pounding heavily and she wanted to die
instead of the lamb or even along with it, never feeling another
thing, never having to lie awake waiting to go to sleep, never
having to eat or drink again. Nothing worse than this could ever
possibly happen to her. How long, she wondered, would a
person have to go without eating to die?

On the way home nobody said a single word except Tolliver.
He chattered to himself from the time they started out. Rachel
kept telling him under her breath, "Shut up. Oh, shut up." He
probably never once thought of the ice chest of meat in the
trunk, and he fell asleep halfway home. Grundy was out of the
Spirit now, as far out of it as she had ever seen him. When he was
not in the Spirit you would think he would get some peace. But

it was the other way around. He would be sadder than sad. He would be the gloomiest man you ever saw. Down in the mullygrubs, Nana said, sighing. He was deep in the mullygrubs now, Rachel could tell by the slump of his body over the steering wheel, and his silence. Nana was leaning against the window, eyes closed, but she was not asleep. Rachel was learning to read them better, quite cunningly sometimes. It was a trick she herself used, pretending to sleep so she would not have to talk to him. They rode endless miles. The sun was gone and massive clouds on the horizon to which they were traveling were flexing their slow, heavy muscles.

"Rachel, you asleep?"

She didn't answer.

"Nana, you asleep?"

No answer.

"Nana!"

She answered him faintly, flatly, like the lamb's bleat.

"Are you prepared?"

"I been ready for it."

"Since it will fall the day after Easter, I think we should wait until Easter Sunday to prepare the children."

"I don't think we should tell them anything. Let them enjoy Easter. We have to pray and expiate our sins, but they are innocent babes. They will be sinless before the Lord and taken up that way." The idea of the Rapture had hit their church and caught on like wildfire. Many were given the gift of tongues, prophecy, and healing. Nana herself had been almost miraculously raised out of her worthlessness and she felt urgings that she had been given the gift of prophecy. She had many messages to reveal, such as a Russian invasion of Germany, the death of Saddam Hussein in July of 1992, and the conversion of China. She prophesied these and other events aloud in church. None of the prophecies came true, and her self-esteem plunged to a lifetime low. Looking back, she should have prophesied that too, since she was too sinful to merit the gift of the Spirit. Neither had the Rapture occurred on the expected date. The new date of annihilation gave her some hope, as death now seemed the only appropriate punishment for her sins and failures.

"Will it be like a fireball destroying the whole earth?" she asked.

"A big flash. You won't know it's happening except for a few seconds. Then it will all be over."

"Praise God."

"When I was nine years old I set my own clothes on fire. And run from myself. Seemed like an eternity but it was only a few seconds. My mother smothered the fire."

Nana looked at his stony profile and it flitted briefly through her mind that he might be crazy. But no, they thought too much alike, and she knew she wasn't crazy. It was natural for death to dominate your thoughts when you reached a certain age. And it was fitting that the End-Time should come now, when the world lay helpless in the hands of evildoers.

"Safe are the blessed in the bosom of the Lord," Ernest said, echoing her thoughts.

"Amen. Rebuke me not, O Lord, in thy wrath, nor chastise me in thy fury," she groaned.

So they were still talking about it, and the day after Easter was going to be the day. You never knew what was going to happen in this world. Rachel did not think her Nana was sinful, but of course, Nana knew best. If Nana had sins... She began to be very worried about herself, because she knew that she herself was in deep sin. It was that she had drawn in almost every library book in the school library. It was something like reading backwards, something she couldn't keep from doing. Nobody knew about it yet. Only one of the drawings had been reported so far, and so the librarian was not overly concerned. Wait until they found out. The drawings were in pencil. Maybe she could erase them starting tomorrow during Library Period. She would have to be very careful not to get caught. It had been so easy to do it. In every book that she checked out and brought home, over the last year, she had done the drawing. Even *Caddie Woodlawn.* She kissed the book cover fervently. She would erase *Caddie Woodlawn* the instant she got home.

The drawing was basically the same: it was usually a man's profile and a woman's facing one another, sometimes a woman's and a woman's, or a man's and a child's. From the forehead of one to the other she drew dotted lines. That was it. Except sometimes there was a word or words on the dotted lines. The words were teeny and did not get very far from the head of the one thinking them. She was grateful to know that she had a week to return the damaged books to their original state—she was an optimist, she knew she could do it—and to prepare herself for the End with prayers and fasting. Fasting would be no problem. She knew she would not want to eat during the coming week, especially would she not be able to eat lamb roast on Easter Sunday.

The weekdays of Passion Week were a swiftly moving cloud of agony marked by uncertainty, fear, and furtive forays into the library at every odd moment of her schoolday. She checked out the limit of books every day—five—and returned the five from the previous day. During her lunch hour and Library Period, a space of only twenty minutes on Monday and Friday, she riffled pages, thousands of pages, in the fiction section. As early as Tuesday Mrs. Kniffin began looking at her suspiciously and she had to be more careful, piling her gym clothes on top of the open page and applying her big gum eraser in tiny strokes of her fingers while she gazed out of the window. Finally Mrs. Kniffin caught her in the bookstacks searching frantically through *Amelia Bedelia* and asked her what was going on. How could she tell Mrs. Kniffin that her eternal soul was hanging in the balance? Like the worst kind of criminal, she had thought out her alibi ahead of time. She told the librarian that she was taking a correspondence course in speed reading, adding a lie to her burden of sin.

The week was awful for Nana and Grundy, too. Nana gnawed her lower lip till it bled. She either walked around and around

the house or sat in her chair near the window. Grundy was high
and low, high and low. He shouted to himself as he did when he
was in the Spirit, but the shouts were like an animal dying. When
he got too low, he went to bed. He missed two days of work, lying
in bed, praying, laughing and crying. Easter Sunday dawned
glorious, a beautiful day, bursting with life, that second-to-last
day of life on earth. Their church service was three hours long.
People were high and low. They hung on to each other and the
preacher, laughed and cried, praised God and sang songs.

Nana cooked, but no one ate much except Tolliver, who
stuffed himself on roast lamb and potatoes on top of speckled
malted milk balls, candy eggs, and a chocolate bunny that he ate
after church. He ate just exactly like there was no tomorrow. He
had been eating that way for several months and he was getting
to be a lovable little dumpling. Rachel foresaw that he would be
a fat teenager. She corrected herself. He would have been a fat
teenager. She stayed awake most of the night, planning tomorrow's final assault on the library.

Easter Monday her grandfather took the day off again. After
some deliberation, Rachel was sent to school. She insisted on it,
because she had not yet finished her erasures and she must find
a way to cover the authors R through Z in a single day, and *that*
only if she was to be allowed to finish the school day before the
End came.

Three o'clock came and she didn't get finished; that is, she
finished the fiction, but there was a scattering of other books she
had read, non-fiction, that she didn't get to. These included
some important, unforgivable ones, like the big *Encyclopedia of
Music*, that she had forgotten about until this very day, this last
day. It was too late now. She went straight home and did not go
out to play with Sheila Neilson. She hovered around Nana who
was in her gray and white print meeting dress. Grundy paced
around the house, stopping once to grasp her and almost
smother her against his stomach and say, "Child, I love you," and
then did the same to Tolliver, who was playing with miniature

cars on the rug. Rachel hugged Grundy back but she did not feel loving to him, had not felt the same toward him since the day they went to Dunk's farm. The eternity of the evening passed, Tolliver fell asleep on the couch. Rachel was allowed to stay up until midnight, then she was sent to bed. She climbed into bed with faintly rising hopes. After all, it was midnight. That meant the day of judgement must have passed. At the very least, she had one more day of expiation in the library. And she could finish it in one more day. She fell soundly asleep. When she awoke the next morning, no one had waked her up for school. She looked outside at the beautiful morning and ran to Tolliver's bed. "Wake up, Tolliver, wake up!" He grunted and turned. "It didn't happen. It didn't happen," she breathed.

They were on the road again later in the morning. Nana had on her gray and white print meeting dress, just as if she had slept in it, and she carried her Bible. Grundy was more grim than she had ever seen him. He had kept her out of school. Although she wished she could have gone to school on this particular day to finish up in the library, Rachel's heart was rejoicing. The End had not come on two consecutive deadlines, and she was beginning to think that it would not come just yet. She had Caddie Woodlawn with her in the car. The hills had never looked so green. The sky had never looked so blue. They passed one farmyard with a clothesline of bright quilts, one with big stars and another with hooked-together circles. Tolliver was singing that crazy song. "Jib jibber-jibber jab and jab jabber-jabber jib!"

Grundy ordinarily did not tell them where they were going, but this morning he did. "Children," he began, grasping the wheel of the car tighter and shifting a little to be able to talk over his shoulder, "the Lord spoke in my dream last night, just as plain as I am talking to you now, and He said that all of us in this family are saved, and that He invites us to come to Him today. He wants us. He calls us to the Kingdom today, for behold now is the acceptable time, now is the time of salvation...." He went

on with some other sayings that tumbled on and on over the back
seat but which they did not understand. "Safe are the blessed in
the bosom of the Lord!" It sounded like his regular self but not
exactly. Rachel listened closer, joy guttering in her heart, but she
could not make out what he was talking about.

"Where are we going, Grundy?"

"Rachel, child, we are going to the Lord." He had to explain it
over and over to them. "We are answering the call of the Lord. It
is time. The time is here."

"How are we going to go to the Lord?"

"Through the dark valley we will pass on to glory!"

"Today?"

"Yes, today, today, our resurrection day! Oh, praise God with
the tongues of angels! Thank you, Lord, for this trial by fire, even
as you commanded Abraham!"

"Praise God," Nana said.

This is not real, she told herself. Nothing is going to happen
to us.

Suddenly Caddie flung herself into Mr. Woodlawn's arms.
"Father! Father!"

It was all she could say, and really there was nothing more
that needed saying. Mr. Woodlawn held her a long time, his
rough beard pressed against her cheek. Then with his big hands,
which were so delicate with clockwork, he helped her to undress
and straighten the tumbled bed. Then he kissed her again and
took his candle and went away. And now the room was cool and
pleasant again, and even Caddie's tears were not unpleasant, but
part of the cool relief she felt. In a few moments she was fast
asleep.

"Is something going to happen to us? Are we going to die?"

"There is no other way to enter blessedness."

Nothing is going to happen to us. Yes, he is going to kill us.
That is what he means. He is going to kill us.

"Massacre!" breathed Mother, laying her hands against her heart. Her face had gone quite white.

"No, Harriet, not that word," said Father quietly.

She opened the book and there was a drawing she had not caught. She must have done two in *Caddie Woodlawn*. A man and child faced each other in profile with faint dotted lines in between with no words on the lines. She rubbed and smudged the drawing with her fingers until it was obliterated and the spot was just a black slur and then a black-outlined hole showing the white of the next page through it. Her eyes were acting funny. The words were sliding around on the pages, then off the pages as she turned them searching for an answer. She went quickly to the last page. The story was over. She was going blind. The last sentence, like an iron bar, hung suspended over half a page of white space. Maybe she could get it off and keep the story from ending. She pried up the last line, bent it upward, but it would not let go. She pulled and it finally snapped off in the middle.

"Nana," she asked, "are you going, too?"

"Yes, Rachel. It's time. We are going to cross over."

"Can't we—can't we think about it some more? Oh, can't we take it to the Lord in prayer?" Please. Please!

"I can't think.... I can't think.... Ernest...."

"Rachel," Grundy interrupted. "Nana and I have chosen this way for her and me. We have made our choice. Tolliver doesn't have a choice because he is not yet of the age of reason but we are sure he wants to go with us."

"I want to go with you and Nana," said Tolliver.

Grundy continued, "You are past the theological age of reason, Rachel, and the Lord commanded me to give you a choice. He compels me under penalty of His wrath to let you choose."

Rachel slid sideways and whispered harshly to Tolliver, "They are going to kill us! Tell them you don't want to go!"

"No. I want to go with Grundy and Nana." He began to cry.

This is not real, she thought. Yes it is. He means to kill us all. "Nana—" She burst into tears and leaped forward to hug Nana's neck. Nana was already turned toward her, and patted Rachel's hair and hands as she cried for several miles. They were now on the main turnpike heading east. Rachel knew this highway very well. She dried her tears on the shoulder of Nana's gray and white dress. "Did you say I could choose?"

"You have the choice of going with us to the Lord or staying behind."

"Go with us, child," urged Nana, with her face shining, not from being happy, but from something like a battle she had finally won. "You will never suffer again. You will be in Paradise."

"Come on, Rachel," said Tolliver, brightening up. "Nana, will it be like Dollywood?"

It would all be over quickly if she went with them. A rip and then blood like a waterfall and she would never have to wonder what was going to happen to her next. She wanted to be obedient to God and her grandfather. God and Grundy merged in her mind. She thought about it for a few more miles in the silence of the humming, hurtling car.

There was that matter of the unfinished erasures. She was certain that if she had to go to God today He would forgive her and give her credit for doing the best she could. She was a logical thinker, even under stress. Her grandmother always said that Rachel had been given the gift of wisdom by the Spirit. But in the end her choice was not made rationally. It was made on the basis of what he had killed when he killed the lamb. That precious pet that in her fantasy she had called *her* lamb, he had killed. Why?

"I want to stay alive."

They put her out on the side of the road with what she knew and with her copy of *Caddie Woodlawn* and her grandmother's Bible.

Mad

The dog was at the gate, biting the air in snatches. The deaf child was watching. A stranger was coming.

Paquet. A dark man, a little old drunken, foul-mouthed tinker, he had turned up one blistering day the year the century turned, had walked upriver from New Orleans on the levee with a pack of pots and pans on his back.

Cassie! Cassie! The name tore out of her throat, bursting out as Unnnngh! and she clutched her apron pockets full of pecans as she ran, terrified. Cassandra, bent over in the pecan grove, straightened up and saw what was coming. "Hush, now. Hush. Umm!—Umph! Here come the devil own right ahm!" She hurried Baby Girl away and forgot about picking up pecans the day that Paquet came.

That wasn't his real name. Anybody who was extra small was a "Paquet," a small package. They might also have called him that because he had disembarked in New Orleans with Gus Wiegand years ago carrying only the bundle on his back. Or, perhaps, because he had come down the levee that day to the Wiegand place, emerged from the dense river haze one morning shouldering the clinking load of pots and pans that made him sound like a one-man band, wearing an ancient Russian sailor's cap, his dark skin underneath stretched like gut membrane over the bones of his face, sweat running into his yellowed mustache that drew flies, Sidonie said, because it was so filthy. Skin and bones, him, Sidonie said. Shiftless. No more to show than what he got off the boat with, and that was damn little. Had drunk it all up, him. Had his nerve to raise hell and expect more than four bits a day, which was not quite what the canefield workers made. But handsome pay for the trifling things he did. And, besides, look how well the niggers behaved and didn't give any lip. Paquet gave everybody hell except Baby Girl.

Gustav just laughed him off, kept him on because of the old bond. Perhaps the old man had done him a favor in the new country, or on the way over. Whatever had been recognizable as human in Paquet, whatever Gus had seen in him at first and perhaps tried to retrieve, had died long ago, had been stomped out like his dead and unremembered youth by liquor, the language barrier, and ill-treatment. He was as expendable as two little nigger boys drowned in the river.

He had been nursemaid to the two Wiegand boys, and ever since they could speak they had made fun of his rags and his gibberish. With Baby Girl it was different. Once he made a pinwheel for her out of palmetto fronds, and she laughed spontaneously, to everyone's amazement. He answered her with "Son of a bitch!"—one of his few English phrases—losing his eyes in the wrinkles of his smile. At this the squirrel walking down a tree waved his tail at her, and trees clapped their hands this way and that. She let Paquet babble right in her face with his liquor breath, and she adored it, ever since he had leaned down and said to her in Hungarian, "Come! Don't hide!" His language made as much sense to her as English. And she knew something interesting was going to happen when he talked in her face. "Dumb can't sing but it can dance, eh child?" he would say to her in Hungarian. Then he would clap his hands, turn, and take solemn high steps, like some stern patriarch, blowing and puffing out his moustaches. She would follow the steps in time, clapping, squealing in delight.

Once in a great while, if she threw herself on the floor and held her breath long enough, she would be allowed to roam with him and the boys. While the boys ran ahead, she and Paquet would dawdle drunkenly in the pastures and woods while he unriddled nameless mysteries for her. His imagination overlaid hers with a bright patterned transparency. He pointed out everything to her, turned all the stones. At night on the back gallery they might investigate a June bug in a spinout under the lantern. In the grove they spied on the jay as he tracked an unsuspecting squirrel and methodically dug up his pecans. They surveyed villages of bee houses, watched the smokestacks of boats moving swiftly behind the levee. If she felt the blast of an approaching river boat, she grabbed at his hand for him to take her to see it.

She remembered the high steps he taught her and did them in front of her mirror. She had an inner loquacity. Not able to tell herself to anyone, she talked to her other self in the mirror, making the shape of Paquet's name, the dog's name, and about fifty other things that she had noticed over and over on people's lips, like the sharp S of Sidonie, and the slack jaw of Gus. ("She'll talk when she's ready," Doctor DeJean was still telling them.)

Now: She and her mother walking hand in hand across the cow pasture, through a back gate, and into the woods on a sun-speckled path where clematis vines snaked up the scrub oaks and luminous moss hung down, seeming to gather the light and glow from within. "Paquet! Awww, Paquet!" Sidonie called.

The girl wore a pinafore, black stockings, and ankle-high shoes. She swung a small tin pail by the handle. She shuffled slightly, dragging the heels of her high-strung shoes. She breathed noisily. Made odd sounds. "She gon' talk when she get ready," the loyal Cassie was still quoting, telling them what they wanted to hear, none of them believing it for a minute. "She be gettin' tired fallin' on the flo' squealing. When she fittin' like that, she be

gettin' herself ready." When the child raged in primal wolf cries
and unintelligible black curses of her own devising, Gus would
lift his spadelike hands helplessly, chide his wife for being too
indulgent with her and bringing on these fits. Sidonie, pepper-
pot French, ignored him. She ran the house and its precincts—
the pecan grove, kitchen garden, back lot, Paquet's woods—the
way she saw fit. Cassie observed, "M'em Sidonie run the men
and Miss Baby Girl run her. O, but she love that baby! Dress her
up like a picture-book."

"Paquet!" Sidonie called again sharply as they approached a
one-room shack. On its unpainted exterior wall of junk lumber,
an orange board here or a blue one there caught flimsy tatters of
sunlight. Under the one shuttered window, a great weathered
red board from the side of a barn said AUGHT, the ghost of
BLACK DRAUGHT. When they reached the wooden stoop,
which was merely a sawed-off, upended tree trunk, the mother
motioned to her child to wait, and took the pail from her, calling
from a safe distance into the open doorframe once again, as one
calls livestock, "Paquet! Awww, Paquet!"

While the mother gave him the wide berth of an unpredict-
able animal, the little girl was not afraid. After seven years, she
and the man trusted each other, understood something of one
another's exile. Now she was ten, not really a child, but dutifully
holding her mother's hand when they went abroad together
because it was what she had always done.

"Drunk!" Sidonie said disgustedly, and slid the pail inside the
doorframe. She seldom addressed the girl directly but the girl
generally knew what her face was saying. "Sent word he had a
fever. Couldn't go out this week." She talked to the air around
Baby Girl. "You hellion! Come on here and get your dinner."
Paquet should have been out in their woods now with her father
and brothers and the others. He cooked for them when they
were cutting down trees. They lived in a shack like this back in
the woods for a long time when they were cutting down trees.
Maybe he didn't go because their dog had bitten him.

Queenie. There had been the dog at the gate, then the dog of that dog, and then Queenie. All of them had always showed their teeth to Paquet. They hated him. Out on the edge of these woods she had seen Queenie bite Paquet. She believed that he had then shot the dog. He kept an old shotgun in his shack. After Queenie bit him, acting like a wild animal, leaping and slashing at him, he had run back to his cabin with Queenie behind him. She was missing now.

"I brought your dinner, you hear—" Sidonie heard a moan from inside. She put her hand briefly on Baby Girl's shoulder to anchor her in that spot, then stepped up into the shack with her skirts tightly furled. Oh, but, yes, he was reeking of liquor, and flung out on his greasy mattress. His face was flushed; he was stupefied, breathing hard. Old hellion.

Like the girl, he did not understand much of what Sidonie said, only how it looked on her face. And this time, he could barely make out her face.

That night Baby Girl, whose real name was Elise, but she didn't know it, thrashed around and around on her moss mattress. It had darked again. Every dark was the same: when your eyes closed you were not anything. So you never wanted to let your eyes close. Never.

Never see a child fight bedtime so…. Buttin' and scufflin' around….

There was no air in or out of the mosquito bar. Not a breath. She struggled to see. The familiar was strange and oppressive. Her goosefeather pillow, blue-white in the night, the bars of her iron bed, the heavy furniture—except for her friendly open-armed rocker in the corner—seemed misshapen, monstrous. Even her favorite plissé gown felt heavy and damp around her body. The shutters, like the outside doors, were fastened but not locked against miasmas with their harmful influences. Closing the shutters also kept out bats and a few mosquitos, guarded the sleeper against the full moon, longing, and madness.

Even if she could have told them about Queenie biting

Paquet, she wouldn't have done it. They would take Queenie's part. They would accuse him of killing her, even if he hadn't. Baby Girl imagined that they might even run him off if they thought he had killed Queenie. They cared more for Queenie than they did for him. Baby Girl herself half-felt this way. She fiercely loved the mute, adoring animal. And where was poor Queenie now?

On the other hand, Queenie had attacked him first. Baby Girl felt both ways about it, and it was a very bad night for her. Good Queenie. Paquet, warm in her heart. She clapped her hands rhythmically in the dark, in a version of Pease Porridge Hot that he had taught her, and threw her palms out to meet his invisible ones. She rocked herself side to side in her customary way, then she drummed her head against the bedstead bars to make her eyes stay open.

She slept late into the morning in her wispy white nightdress that lay like a small collapsed cloud in the middle of the iron bed, as if she herself had evaporated in the night out of her dream-cloud. Cassandra, walking in upon her, tangled and lost in the gown and bedclothes and her own long hair, thought, "Angel." Her forehead was like her father's: stubborn with intimations of the fixed purpose that had driven him to the new world, but innocent and blank. Her eyes were deepset like her mother's, but when they were open they lacked Sidonie's sharp restless scan. They were empty of expression, fixed as in a Daguerreotype.

"Come on, Angel, heist your wings!"

Her waking impression was of Cassandra touching her back lightly between the shoulder blades. She was irritated at this and threw her arms and legs around on the bed, rolling over, glaring at Cassandra and making angry-elephant noises. She was small but gangly, her limbs not nearly finished. Cassandra left her alone. "Miss Baby being quarrelsome this morning," she told Sidonie.

When she woke up again, she was feeling better. She and the black woman raised the mosquito bar and threw it over the top of its frame. Then they folded back one end of the pliant moss mattress, revealing the "springs" of the bed, the shuck mattress. The shuck mattress had to be fluffed every morning through openings in each end. After struggling for a while at one end, they moved to the other end, folded back the moss mattress, plunged their arms into the dusty shucks, worked out the bulges, reshuffling, pummeling, and smoothing out the shucks until the mattress was roughly symmetrical again, or at least, until the lumps were uniformly distributed. They did the same to her mother and father's mattress. They would have given her brothers' beds the same treatment as part of the morning routine, but the brothers had been away in the woods for almost a week now. She didn't miss the brothers. She didn't feel kin to them, never having seen the color of their eyes or their mouths moving at her.

She did not get dressed, testing the women. Her mother looked at her pointedly, ran her hands down her own muslin dress, looked again at her daughter. Baby Girl shook her head pleadingly and her mother humored her, since the men were gone. The child padded barefoot into the kitchen, stretching elaborately, and tried the new kitchen pump, pushing up on the big handle and then hanging from it, her feet off the floor, until it worked up and down easier, and clear, cold water began to gush into the sink. She washed her hands and face, and when it turned icy cold, drank some of the water. Sidonie herself fixed them something "simple," she said, *pain perdue*, for breakfast. She used a stale loaf. She cut it in thirds, then sliced it lengthwise, soaked it in beaten egg mixed with fresh cream, raw brown sugar, and vanilla, and fried the pieces in deep fat. It was freeing to her soul to have the men gone for a while. She and Cassie did not have to fry steaks and make a stock pot of grits every morning before dawn, or cook a big spread for dinner right on the heels of breakfast. She could tend to her little garden off the end of the kitchen gallery, catch up on her mending in the afternoons, sitting in the porch swing. She decided to ease her mind even more and forget Paquet, too, leave him to stew in his own stinking juice as long as it took. She would be switched if she'd bring him his dinner again, she thought, impaling a puffy golden chunk of bread with a two-tined fork as long as her forearm, and lifting it from the black Dutch oven.

Two days went by without a sighting of Paquet. Then two more. On the fourth evening, sewing on the back gallery before dusk, Sidonie wondered if he might be dead back there in the woods. Maybe he really did have a fever. People said that dengue fever—they called it breakbone—was spreading up the river. Maybe she should send for Doctor DeJean—he was a good fever doctor. Maybe he is dead of drinking back there, she kept thinking. Oh, he's slept off many a binge back there. Days at a time he'd be hung-over, full of rot gut. Maybe...she didn't know what to think. Queenie didn't show up either, even when Sidonie brought out her big dishpan and banged it with a wooden spoon, calling loudly to raise them, either one, man or beast.

"Paquet! Paquet! Queenie! Queenie! Queeeeenie!" Her shouts echoed back from the darkening woods. She must go see about him in the morning. She directed Cassandra to stay the night. "We'll go see about him as soon as it's daylight. Now, don't suck your cheeks in like that. I need you here. If they don't see a light in your cabin, they know you are here with me because the men, they gone."

"Yessum."

Hours later, as branches of trees scratched at the rising moon, an unusual sound pulled Sidonie from a deep well of sleep, up to consciousness. She wouldn't have heard it, probably, if her bedroom hadn't been across the hall from the kitchen, overlooking the back gallery. It came from the gallery, or, it seemed, under the gallery. It was a low, snarling kind of sound, and when she first heard it, she rose up in bed and called softly, "Queenie!" Again, harshly rolling sound, constant, from a throat that seemed not to be taking, not able to be taking, breaths. "Queenie?"

She was only to her bedroom door when she heard him burst into the kitchen. It had to be Paquet. Even then, she was more angry than afraid, not especially wanting to wake Cassie. If he's drunk again... She had handled him in the past, she could handle him now.

The noises he was making! From the black hole of the hall she hurried into the moonlit kitchen. His back was to her. He was naked to the waist, staggering forward to the pump, and she noticed at once that he was thin, thin—his back was bony. She had one coherent thought—that she was not altogether relieved that he was not dead, after all—before he took hold of the pump handle and began to rave at it. The water came and he flung himself away from it, coughing out unintelligible words, hurling the kitchen chairs against the walls. She screamed for Cassandra. He turned to her, coughing, drawing air in great sucking, rasping breaths. Then she saw—O JesusGod, all on the sharp intake of breath—froth had gathered on his moustaches. Some had fallen in small puffs, moonlit on his naked chest. He grabbed at her as Cassandra pounded into the kitchen, snatching a broom as she came, warding him off for a moment.

"He's not drunk, Cassie! It's a fever. Or he's gone mad!" They turned and ran by instinct back to the girl's room. He ran too, easily got through the door right behind them. Baby Girl began making high squealing shrieks that drew him to her. Then she saw that it was Paquet. Making steps and clapping his hands? And laughing? Laughing, in the half-shuttered moonlight. He was biting at the air in snatches. She sat up dead still and watched him. Sidonie just managed to drag her from the bed as he threw himself on it and lay there convulsing and choking. She held her hand over her daughter's mouth. Cassandra and the mother looked over the girl's head into each other's faces, wild with the same thought. Rabid.

Cassandra had a mad stone in her cabin. Be no use going there to get it, she told herself. They done be bit up time I got back. She turned and ran back to the boys' bedroom, where she had been sleeping.

"Cassie, come back! Oh, God, don't leave me!"

She came back quickly, dragging a moss mattress. Sidonie grasped the other side of it and they lunged clumsily with it toward the man. He sprang up screaming, wrestling the mattress away, biting and clawing it, trying to climb over it. Their screams joined his on the other side as they threw themselves against the wall of the mattress, scarcely any less berserk than he, possessed with the energy of the berserk. They managed to drive him back onto the bed, against the wall, crouching behind the mattress. They pushed with all their strength and he suddenly gave way, crumpling down on the bed. They climbed on top, panting, still screaming, Sidonie calling for Gustav, as if he might hear her from the farthest woods, Baby Girl joining her high squeal to the man's agonized cries half-stifled under the mattress. Directly on top of him, the white woman and the black in their nightgowns grappled with him in the semi-darkness, clung to the thin mattress as to a liferaft on a heaving sea. He fought for his life. His spasmodic movements were like convolutions, from the sea-floor, of a great demonic worm attempting to surface. They grasped the iron bedstead, hooked their free hands under the siderails.

Suddenly they felt her strong wiry body on the bed. She pulled her mother's streaming hair, howling desperately, trying to loosen their hands. She jerked at the corner of the mattress where she knew his face was, and Sidonie beat her off with her fists. She fought her mother, leaped on her back like a savage. Sidonie threw her off violently to the floor. The girl made two more attempts to pull the women off the mattress. They held tight.

They did not know when he stopped struggling or when his last sounds, or Baby Girl's, ended. Sobbing and praying through the night, they didn't dare get off the bed until daylight, and Sidonie clung tight to the bed even after bright splinters of sunlight fell on the floor. It was Cassandra who threw a shawl over her nightgown at dawn and ran to the cabin road for someone to fetch the men home from the woods.

The girl awoke to the vibrations of feet around her. In the tumult no one thought of her. Her parents were distraught. To her brothers she was essentially invisible. She crawled to her rocker and huddled there in the corner of the room, rocking in a small steadying rhythm. Doctor DeJean, quickly summoned, confirmed the death. Hydrophobia, he said, without a doubt. When they made ready to remove the body, Gustav noticed his daughter, picked her up out of the rocker, and carried her out. She was long-limbed and stiff, like a dead body in his arms. She remained that way while Doctor DeJean gently disrobed her, gnawed at his moustache in suspense, and found no marks on her. "Elise is a fine brave girl."

They hauled her moss mattress and her shuck mattress, as well as the mattress with which they had smothered him, out to the back lot, soaked them with kerosene, and burned them. Doctor DeJean told them, "Queenie might have been the carrier of the disease. Or possibly it was a rabid squirrel or coon."

When he came back in two weeks to check her daughter again, Sidonie told him she despaired of explaining it. "You can't make Baby—Elise—understand," she said. "Why we did it. She sees everything like pictures on a wall. She doesn't understand before and after. I try to act it out, but she's not ready for it, and she screams and runs away. Terrified! Oh, I tend to her so! I keep her close and dress her pretty and cuddle her. But now she's so inside herself, she's turning away her head and pulling away from me. She hates me now."

She caught the doctor's sleeve. "Please, please, explain hydrophobia to her." Desperately, she tore a blank page from the back of Gustav's ledger and handed it to him. He took Gustav's rigid accounting pen and his ink pot, and lifted Elise to his lap at the dining room table. He drew pictures of a stick dog with a mad, vicious look on its face, biting a stick man. The mean-looking stick man, in turn, bit another stick man. All expired, became a pile of sticks. Elise stared at the little scene for a long time. Then she burst out crying—Unnnngh!—swept the paper to the floor, hid her face between Doctor DeJean's vest and his tight black coat.

At night she dreamed of smothering and woke up gasping, but did not make a sound. She felt writhings under her new mattress. So she did not sleep on her bed now. The rest of the summer nights, she took her goosefeather pillow and quilt to the front gallery and slept out there under a makeshift mosquito bar. She became more inward, they all noticed. She ceased to make sounds. They never heard the trumpeting elephant or the old wolf cry that had stood equally for frustration, pain, or, occasionally, supreme delight. They did not hear her squeal.

Gustav thought, "She's growing up."

Her mother thought, "*Là bas*—out there on her sandbar— how can I explain it to her—" the *it* now grown to such imponderable proportions that she could hardly, for all her practicality, see the whole of it. "Will I ever be able to explain? And if I find a way, will it be too late?"

The Proselyte

The Gros Nez settlement lay drooping under the heat of mid-August that hung over it, limp and irritating as mosquito netting.

Guy's mother, Corinne, rocked in the big rocker on the end of her front porch. The opposite end of the porch careened off at an alarming forty-five-degree list, but Corinne rode the peak of the crest valiantly in her rocker. She was clad only in a fiercely flowered kimono—the least amount of clothing a respectable lady could wear on Sunday.

She rocked vigorously, failing to cool herself but stirring up rhythmic gusts of air for her son, who lay on the incline at her feet. The boy had a stack of cards he was sorting into small piles.

"What is that?" she asked him.

"Holy pictures. They passed them out in church this morning."

"How come you got so many?"

"I took them from the back of the church. It's all right. I left plenty there." He held one up. "See?" he continued, not waiting for her reply. "They mostly are Holy Family pictures. These others are Sacred Heart ones. The Holy Families are the prettiest."

Corinne took the gilt-speckled card he offered her and thrust it in the pocket of her kimono. "This'd go nice in my scrapbook." She kept a scrapbook of movie star pictures and magazine advertisements.

Guy restacked his pictures into one pile and rose.

"Where you going?"

"Fishing."

"*Va-t'en, va-t'en,*" she said with an irritated wave of her hand. "Go on. Never mind the crab nets and the shrimp boxes. When is the last time you did something around this place? When?"

"This morning—"

"Yes, yes, this morning. You do something around here and I will publish it in the New Orleans *Picayune.*"

"I'm going fishing. Might pick some moss. That's something."

"'Tam you. You and your papa. 'Tam both of you."

He scrutinized her face, looking down at her tiny, screwed-up features as though from a great height. She wasn't really mad, just talking. He could observe her because his mind was always leaping far ahead of hers, then forcing itself to mark time while she caught up. Now he refocused his eyes upon her until she regained her normal proportions.

"I'll be back after while. Bring y'all a old three-pound cat," he said soothingly, making his exit.

"Be here for supper, you." Corinne was glad to see him go. He had annoyed her all day, lounging around under her feet.

Guy walked straight through the house to the back porch, where he picked up his bait from the ice chest. From the screened *garde-manger* he took a few slices of bread and put them in a paper bag. When he went around the front of the house his mother was still rocking. Her eyes were closed and she didn't see him go.

The white shell road shimmered in front of him. He couldn't look at it, so he looked to each side as he walked. Mrs. Dupain's neat, whitewashed house came into view. Mrs. Dupain also was rocking on her front porch. His family and the Dupain family held a mutual contempt for each other, so Guy unwillingly squinted his eyes and pretended to be thinking very hard when he passed her house. The creaking of her rocker followed him to the bend of the road, where it gradually faded and blended with the Sunday drumming of insects.

In Gros Nez the leaden stillness was unbroken until he reached the Sans Souci Bar. His father and the other men were there drinking and talk, talk, talking about themselves. The old wooden buildings beyond the Sans Souci Bar leaned lazily against each other as though their years of close proximity had made them affectionate. Paul's Feed Store tilted over toward the Belle Theatre, and the Belle Theatre in turn rested against the dry goods store. They looked sad enough on weekdays, when human beings populated them, but on Sundays they were desolate. Only the bank building, which was brick, held itself rigidly aloof as befitted its station. It stared out upon the street through two arched windows which gave it the appearance of having just raised its eyebrows.

The bayou was close by now. He could not see it but he could smell it. The odor of fish and wet vegetation was not unpleasing to him. He walked a little faster, reached his own boat and dropped his bait into it gratefully. Like other craft peculiar to that section of the country, his boat had built-up oarlocks so that it was manipulated from a standing position. He untied it and pushed off from the bank.

When perspiration began rolling down the small of his back, he stopped rowing while he took off his shirt and shoes. He didn't feel like fishing so he rowed on and on, pulling away from the settlement with smooth, long strokes.

The purple water hyacinths opened to make a path for him. They were blooming most profusely at that time of year and seemed about to submerge from their own top-heaviness. He scooped up one of the plants on an oar and watched the stringy black roots rise, dripping, out of the water. "That's how some people are," Hector had told him once. "They pretty like that on top but they slimy underneath." Dead Hector. A year ago, if he had thought "dead Hector," his heart and throat would have stiffened with grief. But he wasn't grieving for his dead brother anymore, merely remembering and curious.

He maneuvered the boat through a small inlet where moss hung over the water like moldy and tattered parade banners discolored by many seasons of rain. A line of turtles on a log eyed him speculatively for a moment, then dropped silently off the log one by one.

"Hey, *tourterelle*," he taunted, "where's your king?" The Turtle King was a mythological beast of Hector's creation whose underwater domain extended over all the swamp. He was only one of a number of swamp beings who had peopled Hector's world. ("When you pass that hollow stump, boy, scrunch down and say three 'Glory Be to the Father's' because Something lives there.")

The swamp had always been a beautiful place, but Hector had made it the green-gold wonder that it was now; had made it that way only for their eyes and the eyes of the few proselytes whom they deigned to receive.

Guy directed the boat toward a particular cypress tree and tied up to one of the knees. He lay down in the boat and closed his eyes, letting his body roll with the gentle undulation. It always gave him a strange, disembodied sensation. He felt he could not lift an arm without a mighty effort.

A leaf fell on his face. Abstractedly, he licked it and pasted it in the middle of his forehead, creating an oddly Cyclopean look on his dark, narrow face. The sun's reflection in the water cast bright, moving spots on his bare chest. He looked, for the briefest instant, not like a human being at all but like an earnest young sprite conjured up out of Hector's head. With his straight black hair falling back from his face, he might have just risen out of the water.

He slept for a while in the shadowed sunlight, then he picked a boatload of moss, which he pulled down from the trees with a long pole.

Late in the afternoon he lay on the moss, ate the bread he had brought with him and watched a heron bend its neck into the water. His eyes drooped. The heron became a lady in a down-soft white robe. He pushed the illusion further and felt a movement like a delicate flutter of wings or a heart beat on his naked chest. She touched her exquisite hand to the arc between his neck and shoulder.

Reopening his eyes, he found only the sun creeping around on his shoulder. He thought of his mother and the other women of Gros Nez and knew then that the heron was only a heron.

It was at that moment that the thought struck him. Hector had been crazy. Absolutely crazy out of his mind. A sliver of fear traveled the length of his spine. A thousand instances of Hector's funny talk and disjointed ways came into his head at once. He had been thirteen when Hector had died—too young and too stupid to see what was under his nose. Hector had had his hand on him like a benediction till now, and now he was crazy and dead and the stump was a hollow stump and a heron was only a heron. The green-gold mystery had lost its sanctity.

He wanted to wail out loud. Instead, a queer sound, a half-yelp, came out and he dug deep and savagely with the oars. A volley of blackbirds exploded from a nearby tree, frightened by the noise. Before he got home, a rank, vapid evening fog had descended, dropping too soon and too unexpectedly, like the final curtain on a beautiful play.

"You spend the day in the swamps one more time and it's too bad for you, yes."

"I'm not going back," he said.

His mother made a half-hearted motion as though she would cuff him with the back of her hand if she had the energy. "'Tam right you ain't. Sit down and eat and then go get me two-bits ice in town. Picou still ought to be open." She turned in the doorway, her resentment not fully spent. "Some catfish you brought back."

He stared at her with a sad perplexity until she averted her gaze. Then he sighed and with his fork slowly made concentric circles through the food on his plate.

"Mamma, Hector was crazy, wasn't he?"

"You never knew that before now?"

"No."

"He was *fou* from the day he was born."

"Are you sure he was crazy?"

"He was born that way. Eat your supper, Guy, for God's sakes."

"He used to talk crazy about the swamp to me. He almost got me believing those things."

"You believe anything, you. Eat, eat," she commanded him. "I want that ice in twenty minutes because your papa bringing some boiled crabs home. Bring me a *Screenland* too. Tell Picou to charge it."

When he got home with the ice and the magazine, they were standing at the kitchen table cracking the crabs. The suspended light bulb swung slowly above them, making a restless nimbus about their heads. They looked like some crude caricature of the Holy Family picture. Mosquitoes and night bugs drawn by the light beat against them. Absorbed in the crabs, they slapped their faces and necks and left thin bloody streaks.

"It's some hot, yes," said his mother, popping a piece of claw meat into her mouth.

His father did not look up. He was swaying gently, almost in the same orbit as the light bulb.

Guy put the ice in the ice chest and the magazine on the sink. He roamed the narrow house restlessly, whistling, fingering objects, sitting in chairs and immediately getting up again.

In the front room, his mamma had a big white conch shell which she used as a doorstop. Someone had brought it from the Gulf Coast long ago. Hector used to sit cross-legged on the floor and hold the pink-lipped shell to his ear. He said he could hear far-off music. ("If you could make yourself small, small and get up in there, you might could hear it like thunder.") Guy heard the music sometimes when he concentrated on it. Now he lifted the conch to his ear and heard nothing but a sound like rushing wind. He covered his other ear and listened and tried to make himself hear it. He could not bear the thought that the music was there inside the delicate walls, forever playing, and he could not hear it. He would rather believe that it was not there at all.

He wandered to the kitchen again and picked at the crabs with his parents, looking sideways, covertly, at them.

"When you catch a nice fish or a big blue crab, you never …well, just look at him for a while before you put him in the box?" He hadn't spoken more than a dozen words the whole day and the sound of his own voice surprised him. It sounded high-pitched and unnatural.

They looked up at him blankly and some shameful sorrow clutched him. He thought at first it was his old grief for Hector returning. But it was not that exactly. He was unable to fathom it. He ached to say something kind to his parents, but not knowing what to say, muttered, "Boy, it's some hot."

Suddenly what he was fumbling for became clearer: his parents had never really been children; not even in some remote past time. Had something or someone made off with that part of their lives? Had they been like this always—sullen, unseeing?

He went to his room and undressed. But the night was too hot and full of sounds for sleeping. Even if he had been sleepy, a mournful bull alligator bellowing in the swamp and the rustling and scraping of a sycamore branch on the tin roof would have kept him awake. The branch sounded like someone sharpening a cane knife on a grindstone. He listened to it with clenched teeth. It was grinding away at his sorrow, filing it to a cutting edge.

He pondered his sadness and remembered other steamy August nights when he and Hector had lain awake and talked; on one memorable night Hector had told him how babies were born. Also couched deep in his memory was that very still, cryptic winter night when they had discussed what it was to die. The night itself had had the cold immobility of death. The only noise had been their harsh, intermittent whispers piercing the numb air. Though they did little to clear up the mystery of why he had to die, Hector's words had awed him. They seemed on the brink of being true.

It was so with everything that Hector said. Guy felt that if the words could be changed about, reassembled, somehow, everything would fall into place. Hector had not really been crazy, he decided, only different. So different.

To ask questions of his parents the way he had asked Hector was unthinkable. He might just as easily hurl obscenities at them; they would be equally bewildered in either case. Maybe they are the crazy ones, he thought wearily.

As he was going to sleep, the bellowing from the swamp grew louder. Lying somewhere in the bottom of his mind was the thought that from now on he would be carrying the burden of seeing partly through his parents' eyes, partly through Hector's, but mostly through his own. When he finally fell into an uneasy dream he heard the old bull alligator on the roof, scratching and scraping with his claws.

Wade in the Water

"I am what I is." This message, in the form of a strong retort from Amelia, caught Vivienne Butler up short and enchanted her all that summer. What did it mean? She suspected it meant that Amelia knew who Amelia was and was satisfied. Sometimes it was less shifty in her mind and more understandable if she turned it around and heard "I is what I am." Either way, the phrase had come from on high, challenging her. It became a secret cachet, a directive to find out that summer of 1956 who she was, as time was running by, summer by summer, and she still didn't know herself. Since they had moved across town, she hardly knew where she was either, but that was second place to knowing who she was.

It didn't help to have all their pictures hanging on the walls, showing every stage of their short lives, from moments after birth to the present. Moon-yene was hanging everywhere, always pretty—she was as pretty as a newborn as she was now at sixteen. And at thirteen, Ronnie Rhett looked the same—unwholesome—as he did as a red-haired toddler with buck baby teeth. He put out more freckles every summer so that they finally smeared, and he got meaner-looking picture by picture. Of all the pictures of the girl called Vivienne, even at her present age of eleven, there was not one that was her very self. She looked different to herself in every picture. The ones of last summer that she thought she had found her true self in, the pictures her daddy took at the recital of Miss Satin Davenport's School of the Dance, turned out this summer to be big phonies. She had been taken in by the bows on the wrists and nylon tulle and spangles and she hadn't noticed her tick-like shapelessness. In fact, in the picture she had adored last summer, all the dancers now looked like a line of ticks in tutus. And she was the roundest tick of all.

"I am what I is, Mr. Bob," was the way Amelia said it when she refused to let Vivienne's daddy pose her for a free portrait, or even a candid shot. The photography studio had been in their cramped-up living room at first, until her daddy had discovered one day, accidentally, a way to lighten skin color in photographs. He could lighten one, two, or three shades. He put out flyers: Butler's Fine Photography—Babies and Wedding Couples Our Specialty. There started to be more and more Negroes waiting in the living room to have their pictures made. They came from Baton Rouge to be photographed. The living room got so busy that her daddy rented a storefront in town for his studio, and they hired Amelia to cook for them. Then they moved from School Street, where Vivienne had been happiest, to Mauna Loa Lane in the new part of town. Amelia had smartened up to the mysterious darkroom discovery (she could hardly not catch on because the family did everything but dance in the streets about it), so that was why she said "I am what I is" and refused to have her picture made.

Amelia and her husband Nance lived in Mud Bottom, the unincorporated part of town by the river that had no streets or alleys to it. ("A place you just walk into," her mother said. "Start anywhere and walk into it.") Amelia was tall and straight up. ("She has a carriage like Ethel Barrymore," her mother said.) But straight as she was, she seemed to have a burden she couldn't lay down.

The Butlers didn't know that it all came from Amelia and Nance's visit to Great-Aunt Doon's, down the river, one day when Amelia was three months gone. The blow came when they were all on Doon's front porch, with her and Great-Aunt Blue talking family history, and it all came frightfully clear to them, from comparing some painful stories of shattered family life, that Nance was Amelia's mother's half-brother. Amelia was married to her half-uncle! Together these two years! And Amelia three months gone with a child!

She had fallen sick upon the news, knowing that the child would be marked (thinking it was only one child), but one night two angels appeared to her in a dream fighting over it and the good angel pulled a sword big as a cane knife and ran the bad angel off, and then laid it on the heart of the agonized mother that everything was going to be all right, that the child would be good luck for her.

She clung to the memory of this dream the rest of her pregnancy, through the very difficult birth of the twins, in which the afterbirth came first, and she hemorrhaged, finally recovered. The great-aunts shook their old white heads. The girls were daughters and "some kind of cousins" to Amelia. But it was all too late now. They might as well all stay together, which they did.

She overworked herself caring for the babies, relapsed, suffered a slight stroke from high blood pressure. Later she lost her sister and her mother. She fell in a ditch and broke her ankle. A few years after that she sat in the first grade of the colored school every day for two weeks with two terrified six-year-olds. The following summer the marked one was bitten by a snake and recovered. Amelia kept clinging to the dream, and now the twins were eleven years old and ready for baptizing, hallelujah, and now, in the Butler kitchen, they were sitting in the corner watching her washing and squeezing a big handful of white rice in a pot of water.

Which she poured off without losing a grain of rice, and then added fresh water, measuring it above the rice halfway to the first joint of her little finger. Vivienne's mother was at the table. Her kitchen shears flashed and worked like a machine. She was brusquely and methodically snipping the heads and tips from a great pile of slender velvety-green okra. It reminded Vivienne of snipping off lizard tails.

Vivienne had been fighting with the snooty Mauna Loa girls all summer. She was cut off from her School Street friends, who were gradually not coming around anymore, so she resigned herself this morning to playing with the twins.

They were mirror images of each other. They did everything the same, when they did anything. Mostly they were very still and shy. They were scared of the same things—lots of things, Vivienne knew from experience. Snakes, nighttime, lizards and roaches, and water, like swimming in water. Vivienne shared many of these phobias. But in addition, the twins had demonstrated they were afraid of dogs, other children, roosters, adults, ants, puddles, cats, crickets, fog, rain, and she didn't know what all. Vivienne couldn't tell what they did like. They never talked, never told her.

The twins had names but Vivienne didn't know them. Very few people did, or took the time to try to tell them apart. Amelia did, of course. And those who knew. Those who knew, knew that one was marked. One had six toes on one foot and six fingers on one hand. The left ones. People knew that to have the left hand and the left foot marked was disastrous. Left anything was a terrible mark to have. The disturbing feeling that the twins were somehow set apart floated vaguely in the backwaters of Vivienne's mind, but she was too young to investigate how and why or to pay much attention to it.

The unmarked twin was deathly afraid of any separation from her sister. The marked twin suffered recurring nightmares in which a snake swallowed her headfirst. Both were soon to be baptized in the river in the last such ancient rite before the church installed a tank. Both were terrified of water.

Playing with the twins was like playing with life-sized rag dolls. Clean rag dolls, not like Vivienne's dirty ones. They simply

sat in a corner till you were ready to take them out and play
ladies with them, p'like they were your babies, or lady friends
with babies of their own, or nurses or secretaries. Making ladies
out of them really wore Vivienne out. If they were her babies,
they needed only to say "Wahhh" or "Mama." But for lady
friends, bridge partners, or phone conversations, she had to
make real people out of them, had to think up things for them to
say as well as her own talk.

This morning they played ladies in her parents' bedroom.
"P'like I'm the mother and y'all are the children," said Vivienne.
The fantasy world promptly unfurled. The word "p'like," Southern contraction for "play like," evoked indescribable pleasures,
instant transport. They were immediately out of body and out of
temporal and spatial concerns, ready to be whisked anywhere
and be anybody that the speaker desired. For it was the
speaker's prerogative—the first one to say p'like—to make the
choice of fantasy. And Vivienne was always the first to say it.

"And p'like we're going to the store. Well, Craig (p'like that's
my husband's name, Craig), well, I'm taking Tashondra and
Tammy (p'like that's y'all's names)...I'm taking Tashondra and
Tammy to the store and you better mow the grass while we're
gone, Craig. Good-*bye!* (P'like we're in the store now and y'all
are being bad.... You have to cry. Say 'Wahh, wahh.')"

"Wahh, wahh."

"Oh, you bad children, you better stop crying.... (Don't stop.)
Oh, y'all are being so bad." She pointed to empty air. "Look at
that little girl over there—*she's* not crying." The twins saw the
white girl not crying. "Do you know the Baby Jesus is looking at
you? He never cried, no, not even once. (Keep crying.)" The
twins kept crying even though they saw the dry-eyed Baby Jesus
looking at them.

"Well, if you don't behave, I'm just going to have to borrow
that man's belt and spank you. (Keep crying.)"

"Wahh, wahh!" cried the twins, filled with wild excitement
and fearful anticipation.

"Well, behave," admonished the mother, relenting, "if you want to get a color TV for Christmas." This time they were allowed to quit crying. "Say, 'Oh, thank you, Mommy.'"

"Oh, thank you, Mommy. Oh, thank you, Mommy."

"Yes, a color TV for your very own."

"Oh, thank you, Mommy."

After they had played ladies and babies and Avon Lady, Vivienne let the twins choose. One of them finally whispered, "Let's p'like we getting baptized." The other one said, "We getting baptized Sunday. In the river."

"Oooo, yes," Vivienne breathed. "A baptizing in the river!" She grabbed the two girls and herded them into the bathroom.

Vivienne's rag dolls were baptized first, plunged in elbow-deep water in the bathtub, with Vivienne as preacher. "A—men! Lordy Lord!" she exhorted. "Brothers and Sisters!"

Then she was their mother watching the twins' baptism. The twins would not get in the tub, however. Next, the twins were spectators at Vivienne's own baptism, at which she also presided. She undressed to her underpants and wound a twin bedsheet around herself. After holding her nose, flopping backwards, and immersing herself, she rose from the water feeling soulfully and ethereally beautiful and pure. "I have seen the Lord!" The twins jumped back, as from a surfacing baby manatee, gave little shrieks and giggles. They played baptizing right up until dinnertime.

Bob Butler came home for his dinner: red beans and rice because it was Monday and washday; meatballs and gravy, smothered okra. The twins stood in the pantry door watching him eat at the chrome and plastic dinette table. Ronnie Rhett (who appeared mostly at meal- and bedtime, to everyone's inner satisfaction), stomped up the back steps and yanked on the back screen door. Their screen door dragged, and instead of lifting and pulling, he simply dragged it open, delighting in the wood-on-wood shriek and shudder. "Hi, Dad." The twins might have been motes in the air. He did not relate to females of any age, color, condition of servitude or consanguinity. "Nyeh, what's up, Dad? Having a good day?" He grinned, teeth as big as piano keys, red hair shocking out for teachers' or for Amelia's itching grasp.

Bob nodded, biting into a meatball. "Pretty good day, son. Pretty good day. Don't drag the screen door that way, son."

Amelia served Ronnie and disappeared through the screen door to hang clothes. Bob looked over at the twins and smiled. "So, I heard you girls are going to be baptized Sunday?"

"Suh," they said softly. They watched him eat. He watched them out of the corner of his eye, thinking how cute they were. He liked to do human interest photos. A baptizing would make a great setting. But he was to be at a photographers' convention in Baton Rouge over the next weekend. As he finished his dinner he thought of Moon-yene. She was plenty smart, handy with a camera, and occasionally helped him out. She could cover the baptizing for him. He went off looking for her.

Ronnie Rhett regarded the okra on his plate. "Looks like a pile of slimy buggers," he declared. The twins craned their necks slightly. "If it was me," he said to the okra, "I sure wouldn't want to be baptized in the river. Get down in that cold cold muddy old water...." He took a drink of milk, gargled it in his throat, pretended to be drowning, grasped his Adam's apple, and then swallowed. "Did you know water moccasins can bite under the water? My dad says they can." He grinned, spooned some rice into his mouth. "See that?" He displayed the rice, then spit it out again. "Their mouths are white inside. That's why they call 'em cottonmouths." He looked over at the girls. They were staring at him, spellbound. He leaned toward them confidentially and didn't smile. "They like black meat."

Sunday was a fine day, perfect for a baptizing. Figs were ripening outside the open windows of the wooden church at Mud Bottom, the community on the river road. Cane was tall already in the fields. Dry mouths were watering for figs and sugar cane.

A mother skunk and her babies slept in a shallow den under a blackberry bush. A canebrake rattler zigzagged slowly through rows of cane looking for a spot to curl up in after the night's hunt. A mockingbird sang in an ageless oak in the churchyard. Banana trees lifted their green fingers of bananas upward, and from the base of the bunched fingers a ringed green stem stiffly descended to a large smooth purple bud hanging deliciously exotic in the deep summer shadows. In the broad-leafed aspidistra bushes that lined the brick pillars on which the church rested, lizards leaped and changed colors. In a rotted-out hackberry trunk in a black hole big as a barrel, something—God knows what—slept the daylight hours away.

The preacher's voice floated out to creation, reassuring it. "Life. Life in abundance. I come to give you life in abundance!" Man Jackson preached a long time, as it was still early in the morning and he was not going to preach at the river. It would be getting too hot then. After he preached, the choir sang "Ride On, King Jesus." The hymn rocked the church and galloped from the open window. Then the congregation of about thirty trickled out, first the preacher and the deacons, followed by the little choir of eight, singing "Wade in the Water," then the candidates for baptism—the twins, another young girl, and a boy—in their white robes and dazzling white headbands. The twins looked up through an old tall pine standing at the corner of the church, the morning sun needling their eyes as they moved in light and shade. Amelia flourished her umbrella proudly in the sun. Nance walked thoughtfully beside her with his Sunday suit coat thrust back and his thumbs hooked in his suspenders. His felt dress hat sat squarely on top of his head.

Moon-yene and Vivienne joined the procession out on the river road. Moon-yene snapped a few pictures unobtrusively, as she had been taught, while they walked along the edges of the procession. Vivienne couldn't keep from skipping.

They passed a Japan plum tree in a Negro yard, Japan plums not yet ripe. Their mouths watered. Cypress vine and poison ivy clung to the fences, green leaves of the poison ivy shading to red on the tips. Nature sometimes gave warning of danger. Flights of irridescent blue mosquito hawks and a few scattered sulphur butterflies hovered around a poison oak vine. Vivienne exaggerated her body around it and the twins did the same. Its orange trumpet-shaped flowers blared a warning that you would be sorry if you touched it. On the slope of the levee to the left, white clover. Bumblebees. On the unpainted picket fence to the right, honeysuckle. More bees. In a web in the honeysuckle a great spindly writing spider recorded something in his zigzag calligraphy. If he wrote your name you would die.

The procession took a turn, went through a gate, climbed the levee. Vivienne especially loved this part of the journey. She liked leaving the known, the roadside, to pretend she was climbing a magical mountain. The traveling troupe walked along the top of the levee, flowing with the river just beyond it, the river swollen in the June Rise. It followed a path along the top of the levee on which everyone walked because it was safer than walking on the road, a path that would be overgrown, closed over in days if it were not in frequent use. A single traveler was coming their way. He was an old, gaunt black man carrying a cane knife, with a beagle trailing behind. He lived back of the levee, some said. Old man and beagle joined the group.

At a certain spot they descended on the other side of the levee. Down they went, at a place only the older members of the group could determine, since it grew over with vines and tangle for being used only once a year. The leading edge of the group, the preacher and deacons, thrashed aside the vines and weeds for the others to follow.

The twins held each other's hand tightly. Blackberry bushes raked their robes with their stickers. Snake places. They saw snake spit on the ripening berries. Vines, bushes, more lizards. Johnson grass and Jimson weed. Fuzzy caterpillars. On cattail rushes in a marshy place near the river the girls saw herds of devil horses, giant black grasshoppers that clung to the stems and ate the rushes greedily, munching with rhythmical jaws. By the riverbank, a few sycamores. The place was thick with willows draped halfway up with vines. Vines everywhere. Snake places. A leafy twig brushed against the marked twin's neck. She let out a piercing scream. Her sister answered her scream, and two deacons carried them the rest of the way.

There was a gentle embankment that even old folk could descend. Their shoes squished in the mud. The baptizing took place where it had for eighty years, in a pocket of the river where only little wavelets ventured in. The inlet was embraced by the satiny morning glitter of the great river. Far out and wide, the river was very fast and full with spring floods cresting at twenty-eight feet. The blue sky over it seemed to be packed and overlaid with unseen, unheard starry hosts of bright spirits casting their reflections on the water in billions of spangles. Vivienne gasped when she came upon it, although she had seen it innumerable times.

Man Jackson and the deacons waded out to their hips. The preacher was in his black robe, the deacons in suits of no particular color, no particular style. Poles had been thrust into the mud to guide them. The preacher began the rite, the candidates stood in line and moved into the water by turns. He baptized the first two and each one came up screaming.

"Thank God for Jesus!" the preacher cried. His shiny face was the color of eggplant.

"Amen!" they answered.

"Our Lord is able!"

"Yes, He's able!"

"We been freed from the power of darkness! We will be a new creation, called the children of God by adoption. We receive in baptism the power of adoption by which we cry, 'Abba! Father!' Do you believe it?"

"Yes, Lord!"

In the general clapping and commotion a new sound suddenly seared the air: overlapping high-pitched screams that sent a group of the women and children running back up the levee through the dense weeds. They turned and saw the old black levee man's arm coming down swiftly with his cane knife in a sure, flashing arc near the twins' feet. Those nearest the center of the scene, still screaming, saw the body of a great snake flopping and writhing. It jumped, rose, and fell on its own severed head. The jaws jerked open once and snapped, the open slitted eyes stared at them. The people's eyes were fixed on the sinuously moving yellow diamonds on its back and the rattle on its tail. Before the diamonds even stopped rippling, the old man had snagged the body onto the hooked tip of the broad, flat machete, and held it high.

"Ohhh," the people gasped, creeping closer. It was a six-footer.

"This is the Lord's day," the old man declared. "Can't let no snake strike on the Lord's day."

Amelia had shrieked when she saw the snake, and crumpled in a faint. Ladies revived her with cardboard church fans shaped like ping-pong paddles, and a little river water on her face. She scrambled up, praising the Lord, and gathered the twins to her. "Oh, children, get in that water, get in the Christian fountain!" "Amen!" everyone answered high and low, and the twins, full of terror, but now seeking salvation in the water rather than on earth, clutched each other and cautiously moved into the river. They seemed two saplings rooted so close together in the same earth that although their trunks were separate, their roots intertwined inseparably in the earth and their leaves trembled, whispered the same pleading to heaven. The water moved up fast as they were guided hand-to-hand—guided quickly on purpose so that they would not have too much time to get scared. But they were shaking. The water supported their weak knees, otherwise they would have sunk down and refused to go on. When they were breast-deep, Man intoned, "I baptize you..." The sisters were submerged simultaneously by two deacons because they would not let go of each other. Vivienne gasped, pulling in the mudsmell of the river, and held her breath with them.

"Latisha!"

"Patricia!"

Called by name! When Latisha and Patricia broke the surface of the dirty water they were not clinging to the deacons. They were screaming and waving their arms like the others had done. Vivienne expelled her breath: "Hurray!" It flashed through her mind: They used to be someone else, and now they know who they really are.

Moon-yene was laughing so hard she could hardly hold the camera straight.

"Moon-yene! Shut up!" Vivienne hissed.

"I can't help it! It's...so...funny!" She stifled herself with difficulty. Vivienne herself couldn't help giggling. Between bouts of laughter Moon-yene kept taking pictures. Her laughter subsided but it stayed on her face mockingly. They were sweating like crazy in the mid-morning heat. Moon-yene's armpits felt as though they were greased. Vivienne's upper lip was stippled with perspiration and her hair was damp, but her mind was totally unaware of her body. Gradually she apprehended that suppressed emotion was making her have to tinkle. That was their family word for it. It was giggle, shiver, wiggle, a St. Vitus dance of joyful agony, a saint's ecstatic pain, for she was having a glorious time in this place with these people. She dashed behind some willows, pulling Moon-yene with her, and together they stamped the weeds down to thrash out any snakes that might be there. Why did she feel so grand? It was the grip of the real. Real as the river. Real as the plumbless horror of the snake. Rag dolls, play ladies, and play secretaries vanished. Those playthings were no longer make-believe of the real, she understood, gasping and shuddering in relief as she squatted and flooded the ground behind the screen of willows, but make-believe of make-believe.

Moon-yene finished shooting her second roll, slung the camera over her shoulder, and hustled Vivienne home to their belated Sunday dinner.

Latisha did not notice until she got home still wet, undressing, that she had the right number of fingers and toes. She counted them over and over. She held her hands up in the mirror and counted her fingers in delight. In the mirror her mouth laughed at herself. But her eyes looked at herself as if they had seen something.

The day after the baptizing Amelia could not withhold even from white people the wonderful news. "When she went in the water she had twenty-two fingers and toes, and when she come out she had twenty," Amelia said flatly and secretly exultant and emphatically. Vivienne's mouth dropped.

Later, Moon-yene said, "Pooh! Amelia and Nance probably had 'em cut off and claimed it was a miracle." She spun a seamless web of total probability around Vivienne. "How come nobody noticed it right away?" Vivienne said she didn't know. "I would have noticed it right away if it was my own fingers and toes. Don't you think you would have noticed it right away?" Vivienne said yes. "I wonder even if she had six fingers on one hand. I never noticed that. Did you?" Vivienne said she couldn't remember if she did or not. "Did you ever notice her feet?" Vivienne said no. "There wasn't any miracle."

She had lots of questions to ask. No one was explaining it to her. She told herself that at the end of summer she would make up her mind. What she came out with, she knew, would be what she was going to think as far ahead as she *could* think, maybe even her entire life. Either every single thing and every single person would be a set-apart self as they were on that June day which had contained all that was possible—or they wouldn't: people would be just people, not marked or unmarked, lizards not able to change colors at all, you never saw them change anyway, it happened so fast, maybe they were two different lizards all along; the levee just a hump of dirt, the river a stretch of dirty brown water that you wouldn't walk out of your yard to go see.

The photos from the baptizing were very professional, her daddy said. When Vivienne saw them she recognized herself with a thrill. She knew where she had been that day—and who. She begged a set of the pictures from her father and carefully arranged them in a brand new album labeled "The One and Only Baptizing."

She wanted to talk to Amelia about the whole thing. Only Amelia could make it all clear, as only she could draw out a stinger from your foot without pain. But where Vivienne had, before, been on equal terms with Amelia, even superior to her in some ways, she now was unaccountably shy. Amelia was not Vivienne's anymore, she belonged to herself. Latisha and Patricia were each somebody different, each one marked in a new way.

Then, suddenly, a month after the baptizing Amelia quit them to cut cane. On Amelia's last day Vivienne had three screaming fights with Ronnie Rhett, one before breakfast, and two between breakfast and dinnertime. She didn't touch her breakfast and ate only part of a doughnut at noon. When Nance came to pick up Amelia, Vivienne insisted on carrying Amelia's string bag. She cried all the way to the car, not wiping the tears, not caring about the way she was sobbing. Only propriety kept her from going to her knees, grabbing Amelia's skirts, hanging on, and begging her to stay. Amelia snuffled a little, too, squeezed Vivienne tight, told her "Goodbye, Sugar Pie," and climbed into the car.

Vivienne didn't see any of them again. When school opened, Latisha and Patricia went to their school and she went to hers. The day she entered sixth grade, she broke away from Ronnie Rhett's teasing half a block away from J. S. Meaux Elementary and ran to cluster with her friends from last year. They were giggling, talking all at once about who was wearing lip gloss. Most of them were wearing it, but not Vivienne. They were checking out five-and-ten jewelry, ribbons, pom-pom shoestrings—and new boys. Vivienne joined in the chatter excitedly. Her eleventh summer fled into an old woman's dreams.

Syzygy

Today I will call Father Blouin to read a Mass for Theodora on the fifteenth. That will be a Sunday. Maybe he will sing a High Mass. She would like that, with music and a soloist.

Her speaking voice, surprisingly small and high like a little girl's, always brought a smile to her audiences after those soaring A naturals. Hers was a little-girl voice and Strechman's ranged from contra-bassoon to oboe, but no higher. He made only gentle sounds. His instrument was the viola. Strechman, gentle as a Tibetan monk. I remember overhearing him tell my mother, "I was deaf until I heard her sing."

Musicians marry one another, you see. It's what they do.

My voice was more clipped and firm, as I think about it. But, then, mine was not in any way a trained voice. I needn't make an apology for it. I apologize too much. I have other talents, there is a stratum of meaning in my life. My husband. My children. Life is a trade-off. I believe I gained more than I lost.

Strechman and Theodora didn't speak English much of the time. They spoke music. English was their second language. They roamed the thickets of the Music Building speaking in the dialect of diapason, which encompassed all of music.

I cannot remember a time segment in our early life in which Theo was not singing. I hear us in a July Fourth pageant, singing the songs America's children have always sung. I hear the charming childish break of our voices in the higher registers of "America, America, God shed His grace on thee...." I'm sure Theo's voice was steady and pure on that first "America." I used to picture George Washington sitting in on our assemblies, listening to us with approval. I think he, or any President, could have learned something from her singing. It was so pure.

More often than I was called by name, I was called "Theodora's twin."

So that the parents would not hear, break it up, we sisters fought soundlessly, wordlessly, pinching and grasping hair and pinning one another down on the upstairs playroom floor, or in the piano room downstairs. When we made up, we would be closer than ever.

On rainy days we lay on our stomachs on hardwood in the piano room. We would flip pages of a shared magazine. As we flipped we claimed possession of either the left or right page according to the lure of the object presented on the page. "I-want-this-nailpolish," I would say, slapping my hand down on a page just as her hand came down on mine.

Turning the page: "I'm this girl!"

"*I'm* this girl!"

Our hands would scuffle briefly in a kind of arm-wrestling duel over the page. I would usually win. I would claim the model with the now-crumpled lips. But Theo would finally win the magazine game by the simple expedient of losing it. Losing interest, she would walk away, humming. Nothing made me madder. I would continue to flip the pages, but since everything in the magazine now belonged to me, it was no fun.

As easily as Theo's breath was drawn in, song came out. Maybe that time she had jaundice and was seriously ill for weeks, she didn't sing. I'm sure she didn't. We were about thirteen years old. My mother moved her into their bedroom. My mother gave over her own place, her own bed to Theodora. Theo's face turned colorless, then yellow, her hair hung lank and dull, breathing was all she could manage in that great bed, big as a warship. She endured rather than fought the illness until she gradually got over it.

I see her on a school stage or to the side of an altar. When she sang the *mus* of *altissimus*, our hearts struggled for release. I see her in a hushed room, a small chamber, a fitting resonator. She is standing next to a piano, my mother is poised to play, or later, Dr. Gottfried, or the music department accompanist. Theodora rests one hand on the black polished body of the piano, fingers touching base with it lightly, her head tipped to the side, listening, lips parted to sing. She is a slim pitcher from which the liquid music would be poured. Strechman would always be at her university recitals. She wore his Mu Phi Epsilon pin on a neckchain.

First he was Theodora's, then I took him away that night on the levee.

Theo and I always loved and hated the same things. We loved and hated and were allergic to the same foods. Our bodies, calibrated to identical biological time clocks, turned on the same gears. Although we purposely varied the surface details, our dress, our friends, our activities, the way we wore our hair, it was futile to fight our twin-ness. People said we even tossed our heads the same way, letting our hair fly right to left, cut short or long. I knew the variable here: Theodora flipped her hair when something was eating on her, when she was perturbed, to shake her brains, to clear her vision. I always did it out of exuberance. We could easily pass for one another, and we sometimes did. She would sit in study hall—and study—for my transgression of cutting up in class; I would take her place at a tea or a social event where our features were not well known. They would say, "Theodora, I've never seen you so lively!"

He, Strechman, was the first boy either of us adored. Until John Mark Strechman, neither Theodora nor I had even liked smooching.

I rationalized that I was her stand-in that night we ended up on the levee—she was singing in Shreveport that weekend. She said, "Let him take you dancing Saturday, Tonia," and I was delighted to be a stand-in, and he seemed happy to have me be one. He and Theodora were tacking dreamily toward marriage, after a courtship of two years. That was a singular quality about T. She was dreamy. Strechman was passive, and so they drifted along together. I think now that I provided John Mark with things he lacked in his genetic make-up: drive, practicality, a way that I have of restlessly searching out the truth of things, no matter what the cost. Something imprinted in base cellular matter desires something lacking in its cellular counterpart, quite apart from the desires of the flesh. John Mark needed me. No one can ever dissuade me from that fact. He needed me. You trade off. I believe he gained more than he lost.

It was a misty, mysterious night. We were triple-dating with Cherie and Paul and Rhea and Bob, parked on the levee after dancing all night at several clubs near the campus. If not now, when? I thought. The others in the car were in place for a programmed set of sweet deep kisses and no heavy petting. It was a wild, free, and gamey spirit that had seized us after the music and the dancing, never to be shared again with him, I thought.

Impossibly, there were no mosquitos, those super spoilers of Louisiana lovers' lanes from time immemorial. It was unusual, too, in that one member of each pair of us was head over heels in love with his/her date. I mean, it's usually just a date, take it or leave it, but there was that undeniable longing in me for John Mark, of Paul for Cherie, and of Rhea for Bob, that made even more magic—it was crackling one to another among us that night. Rhea was my best friend and she was also John Mark's cousin. The conversation was on overload, every word, sigh, and phrase freighted with hidden worlds. Every joke the funniest ever told and every laugh on the verge of hysteria.

Then, downriver, the moon came through the mist. She lost him to me then, at that moment, my serious, cerebral Theodora, her thoroughly transparent gray eyes glancing from the first to the last row, and back again. Her concentration would be total, consuming every faculty, her fingers would be on the piano, translating the vibrations like Braille.

My fingers could not touch him enough, the hair of his head, the pulse of temples and throat. *Hud* was playing everywhere that summer. We always thought he resembled Paul Newman, with dark brown crinkly hair and clean looks and intense eyes. "I love you, Tonia. I love you. I'm sorry," he whispered over and over. "I love you. I'm sorry. I'm sorry." There was the sound of soft kissing all around us. It was driving us mad. I kept touching with my fingertips those miraculous places around his clipped curly hair, his clean, tight-skinned skull and pulsing throat, and then began kissing those places, and then his lips.

All too soon, but maybe just in time, Paul started the car and turned on the lights. He swerved the car around and down the levee road. We all rolled sideways in the back seat, Rhea and Bob laughing and protesting the move. And Strechman: "No, not yet. C'mon Cuz, let's don't leave yet." But in moments we were chasing down the moon on country roads, on the way back to the campus. The others were deliriously screaming or shouting on their way back. But not my love and I. We could not kiss long enough or deeply enough. It was as though we were on our way to our deaths.

Our life of double deceit began then. It wasn't hard to do, logistically, for a time. Although we three were juniors, we lived apart off-campus, sat in different classes, ate and drank at different spots with different friends. Theodora was always in rehearsal for something. Or practicing long hours just to get ready for a rehearsal. Strechman became someone else. He surprised and disappointed me sometimes, how he lied to her and distorted reality as adroitly as he fingered strings. My own machinations were drowned in his. Everything in me drowned in him. His lovemaking was vicious—I was ecstatic to experience it—and in return I exacted every pound of flesh that was mine.

His flesh was mine, the golden dagger that repeatedly stabbed me. I had a right to it. What we were doing tore us apart and flung us back together again like conspirators.

The first time we tongued one another, when I began with his ear, it was her tongue I tipped teasing into his ear. I had seen for myself what her lips and her song did to his hearing. Now I saw the whole love affair between her tongue and his ear. Saw I could not stem that tide for long. I was merely a variation on the theme of Theodora. Musicians marry one another, you see. It's what they do.

But I would fight that. He could forget song. He would not forget my body. The most malignant thoughts rose in my mind at our most tender moments. I would kill him before I let her have him.

This was the time we learned what tongues could do. I could not imagine he had ever done this to T, or, more to the issue, that she had ever done this to him. She was too delicate, my sister of incredibly refined sensibility, she who could turn a pratfall into a graceful glissade. Now we were far beyond delicate tipping with our tongues. We were in stages of exquisite struggle, the first stage a torture for the sake of which we would gladly lose our souls, groaning GodGodGod. In the final stage we were bawling beasts.

Once, after being with Theodora (over which I cried for a week), he said to me, at least seventeen times, "It's over with her, it's over." Then, "Love is not heaven when it hurts like this. It's from the God-damned-est part of hell. Nobody—*nobody except God*—is worth this turmoil!" A minute later we were each by turns kissing and caressing the flesh of the other in delirium. *Do you love me? You must love me. Me. I want you. I. I want—*

It was only a matter of time before someone, probably Rhea, my best friend from the night on the levee, told on us.

Theodora and I had a confrontation of sorts. Unlike me, Theo could not confront. "Oh, Tonia. Oh, Tonia," was mostly what she cried over and over. (I think she also actually said, "How could you?") She was motionless throughout. I never saw her stand so immobile, crying, "Oh, Tonia!"

It wasn't my fault, I told her. It wasn't anyone's. I still think that, and I am not one to dodge responsibility. I have always been one to try to get to the truth of things. All I could say at the end was, "Didn't you always know we would someday fall in love with the same man? I knew." It was not said in triumph or derision. It was said in some kind of sudden self-surprise. I could see so clearly the truth of it: The physical event did not happen. It was already there. We merely encountered it.

She tossed her hair like an automaton and turned away, bewildered rather than enraged. The real impact would hit her later, I knew. She would never turn her face to mine again.

Our parents knew nothing. What did they know, anyway? They lived in the glowing myth that youth is a golden age. They were sinfully proud of their daughters. Our mother, who gave piano lessons, was especially proud of Theodora. She favored Theo implicitly. She couldn't help it, although she tried to hide it.

Our mother gave lessons in the piano room, a natural echo chamber. It was our mother who called it the drawing room. We used to tease her that all it ever drew were mice. It was empty of everything but the grand piano. "We may not be rich," our mother used to say, "but we have a Rolls-Royce in our drawing room."

The house is Charles Addams Gothic. It looks even today like anything—anything—could have happened there. Things of unspeakable anguish. *Do you love me? You must love me. I want you. I.*

John Mark and I have lightened its look considerably by painting the grillework surrounding the portico a pale pink— yes, pink—and the copper hoods like ugly ski-jumps over the narrow upstairs windows, they are pink, too. They used to be black. The brick of the house was red to the point of black, and the sharp roofs, the black copper-sheathed roofs, the black-green leaves of giant magnolias in front that shut out all light, made it the most forbidding place you could imagine. We have lightened it considerably. The magnolias continue to produce prodigiously. Their great blooms, in April, are creamy white and smooth as skin, waxy.

A lingering residue, perhaps from his interest in music, turned Strechman toward math. He is an accountant, a CPA who makes a very secure living for us. Figures are dispassionate. But they add up. That is why he loves them. A column of figures in a printout has no real meaning, just as a bar of music or a staff full of notes on a sheet mean nothing to me. But the figures add up.

Our three children loved this house. They laughed and roughhoused in the playroom, or spent quiet and happy hours there with their books and toys. They are grown and gone now. We sold the piano long ago. I have followed an interest in home decor. I design interiors for homes and offices. Can you imagine what it's like for me to live my life out in my hometown, to work here alongside the families I grew up with? *You're going to live in the house?* Implying, *What does John Mark think of that?* Implying, *How could you? How could you?*

There is some mobility in the town, of course, there are new people. But the old people talk to the new people. They get acquainted. The new people learn what the old people know. Did you know that she is a twin? No, I didn't. Yes, there's quite a story there....

Of course. We are going to renovate. The drawing room's perfect for his office. I wanted the children to grow up in this house. I said to him, "Plenty of room in this house for all of us, and the old piano room's perfect for your office." (Except for our mother, within the family we always referred to it as the piano room.) Why shouldn't I say such things to him? Why shouldn't I? He would not speak of it for so long, while I was mad to uncover, uncover.

Why do you think it is somewhat obscene that John Mark and I sleep and have sex in the same room my parents did? yes, in the same bed, the bed of Theodora's jaundice.

Some years after he installed his office in the piano room he stopped the pendulum on the grandfather in the hall, disengaging it entirely, resting it in the bottom of the clock waist. He said the pendulum bothered him. He didn't like its "swollen look." Why, after years, would it bother him? The clock did sound hollow, hearing it from the curtainless piano room. It never bothered me because I shut out the sound. I never looked at the clock. I added carpeting, paneling to the room. Drapes to the tall wooden shutters. But the clock was down and it stayed down.

John Mark is attractive. More than ever. It is impossible to be sexually indifferent to him. He keeps a year-round tan, from tennis. Most of his free time is taken up with tennis. The game preserves the legs of his youth, those smooth, flat brown planes of his thighs. People like to believe, I'm sure, that he has a secret sorrow which makes him look so grave, so charged with feeling. Men and women empathize with him. But I tell people the simple truth: It's genetic. All the Strechmans grow extremely handsome with age.

Tell me that you love me.

Yes, I love you.

Did you love me at the start?

Wanting and loving are the same thing when you are young.

What about now?

I want you and love you.

Now? This moment?

Yes.

Sometimes I would make a joke. "Strechman, you don't add up." If I didn't love him so much I would have declared him not worth fighting for, years ago. He makes me angry enough to hit. I have hit him. Many times. After which I realize how he has loved me. Endured with me.

The grandfather is across from the mirror. If only time were one-way. We think we possess it in clocks. We are the clocks. Two-way clocks, ticking forward and back. Did the pendulum remind him of a metronome? He stopped winding the clock long ago. Was it the ticking, the striking? Why did he want it to run down?

Does a song exist when it is not being sung? The last thing I ever heard Theodora sing was a piece called *Vocalise*, by Rachmaninoff, I think. There are no words to the song. It was "Ahhhh, ahhh," all the way through. Strechman didn't go to this recital. It sticks in my mind, that melody. A strange, haunting piece, no words to the music. We still have the tape.

Directly after this concert, her junior recital, Theodora quit school. We always thought she went straight to New York, and time proved us right. Gottfried, her voice coach, was beside himself. He came to me and told me she was leaving school. Couldn't I do something with her? "She's a potential *soprano assoluto*, everyone knows that. By that I mean she's at home in any role and any style. She can master the most difficult material, in relatively short order, too, she can get it in the voice. Have you ever heard her mention *nota filate*?"

I shook my head.

"She has that spun tone." Seeing my incomprehension, he threw up his hands. "It's a gift. It's excellence. It represents a high state of technical excellence. What can I say? She has such great musical instincts—"

"We don't communicate now, Dr. Gottfried," I said. "She doesn't communicate with any of the family. I think she doesn't want to take money from the family anymore. She probably wants to get a job on her own in New York, or wherever she's going."

"I can give her the highest recommendations, of course. But she should never, never be leaving now without her degree. We were just prepping her for the south-central Met auditions. She has a future. Or had. I told her she would be crazy to leave."

I had a distinct vision of T's face. She was always elusive, never confrontational. She didn't know how to be retributive. It wasn't in her nature. It wasn't like: You did this thing to me so I am going to do this thing to you. Instead, I saw her mouth saying to me, "I'm gone, even as you speak." And so it was. She disappeared from our screens in spite of all our fine tuning.

My father and I flew up east to look for her. My mother begged to go, but I said, "If she goes, I'm not going." We had had a break in our relations at that time. I could get along with my father. He lived his life and I lived mine. He never invaded our lives like our mother did.

We thought she must be looking for work as a musician. I thought, more realistically, she might be selling cosmetics in a department store. She was an expert at make-up. We tried all the logical places.

New York is a cold Mother. Under other circumstances, say, if John Mark and I had been there on our honeymoon, it could have been intoxicating. But New York can eat a woman alive, especially someone like Theo. For weeks we slogged along all the predictable streets, especially in the theater district, squeezed out with all the others in the moving, oozing stream of flesh, as from a pastry tube. We tried all the big stores, the big-name beauty houses—Lanvin, Chanel, Estée Lauder—the little parfumeries, piano bars, hotel lounges. We asked them if they knew a woman.... We didn't need a photo. "She looks like me," I said.

We investigated every voice coach's ad. Every day we went out to meet hot sickening aromas from the food joints. Was she eating? Was she eating in one of these? I scanned every face, the faces of people in elevators. My father read the papers, obituaries, afraid he would see her name there. It was an unavoidable fear when you dealt daily with the human and mechanical flux. Drugs. Muggings. Rapes. Traffic. Steel. Concrete. Glass. Granite. Aluminum. Chrome. Neon, even in grim daylight. Down close, cast iron. Closer still, grease, gum, scum, tar, dried vomit, snot and lung slugs, black blood, or was it fruit drink, in a drying stream across the sidewalk. Twisted steel skeletons, rock piles, sticky fast food floors, unidentified shit, battered flesh, ratty pigeons. Meanwhile, the muscle memory faded, the diaphragm weakened.

At night, near the theater district, in the bright lights of the pitiful little shops, rubber novelties dangled from the ceiling, bobbled around and fondled one another. In other dives that were like caves, there were other choices. Live Nude Models. Private Fantasy Booths. Video Peeps—a quarter. We asked about Theodora on these streets, too. We left our name and address everywhere.

We came home. Four years later we received a note from an anonymous someone that Theodora had been in New York and had now moved to L. A. They even gave us an address. We were unable to locate her by telephone, so my father and I again climbed on a plane. We went directly to the address given us. It was a bad area. The house was a 30's double bungalow, being used as a commune. No one was talking at first, and they never would admit they knew where she had gone. Perhaps they really didn't know. In the life of the times, drifting anonymously in the tide was what you did. And you finally were sucked West and, without once looking back, you entered the maelstrom of California.

One of the hippie men—his manner told me, "Sure, I used to go down with her all the time"—finally relented and told us that—there—that battered car out front was hers. It had broken down and she had abandoned it there. There was nothing in it except a bra in the trunk.

It was impossible to exorcise this memory. When my father and I got home I wrote in a notebook. *You're gone now, Theodora, you've taken your body somewhere else. I can't find you and, God knows, I've tried. Everyone has tried to find you, in order to be able to either rejoice or start forgetting you or, barring that, to carry on, bearing the daily psychic pain and guilt, hoping and praying that you will make contact one of these days. In time, the others have come to think that your body has no more story to tell. But I continue to live out your body's story. Hearts cannot hurt, they say, but receive referred pain from other sites in the body. My heart hurts from the body blows you have taken.*

I was glad John Mark had not seen what I had seen. I didn't tell him a lot, either about our search, or my feelings about our experiences. Theodora had surprised him so thoroughly by disappearing (he didn't know her as well as I did), he was thrown that much closer to me. He depended on me and I on him. We sustained one another.

It really was like death. If you untwisted a double helix. It was final, all right. Theodora and I and Theodora and he were like lovers torn asunder. Lovers, after the love affair. Every joy was tinged with her. Every happy event had its sorrowful counterpart in the past, doubled. It was the love thing applied to twins: Our song, the one we sang constantly. Our toes: their funny configuration. Our bedroom corkboard, cluttered with mementos. Our cat Eliza.

Strechman eased the pain. Considerably. He was mine, after all. The love thing became ours. Our star, our poem, our this and our that. We had to be careful to avoid the Our Things that had been Theodora's and mine or Theodora's and his. It was as though she had carefully laid a minefield through our love route before she left. Music blew up in our faces: counterpoint. Or a particular double rondo by Bach. I don't know how it's listed, but I know it when I hear the first notes. We could not listen to sopranos. I could not listen to the viola, his instrument, with its vibrato, warmth, intimacy. Even now, I cannot bear to hear sopranos or strings.

When did you fall in love with me? What made you fall in love with me?

Vocal cords enlarge over time. This is a plus for a singer. Her vocal cords were enlarging. Perhaps she met someone. Musicians always find one another.

I would dream, then I would act out the dream with him. *When did you fall in love with me? What made you fall in love with me? You know you still love me.* In his oboe voice he says, *I do.*

Occasionally I break out from eating shellfish or tomatoes. There are many other little red tongues of remembrance that flick out and burn. For example, when I used to have my period. Thick blood. Ten times thicker than water. Our blood gathers on our birthday, January 15. Janus. The celebration of my birthday on January 15 was for many years a terribly oppressive event for the whole family. We finally abandoned it. Of course, they wish me a happy birthday, they give a little gift, but it is not the big event it once was.

Theodora materializes also when I pray. And I often do, surprisingly. Theodora and I had prayed together out loud as children at bedtime, taught by our grandmother. I have even prayed to lose my memory, both short and long-term, because the short-term, while it does not store her, stores memories of memories.

The first child was a girl. The obligation evaded, unthinkable, to name her after Theodora. Theodora had hated her name, anyway. Theodora no longer existed. Except, in our children, when they were young, I saw Strechman and touches of her that are not me. Zoe tossing her long hair in confusion. A strong lyric voice in the boy.

Her silence pressed on my ears. It was like lead shot pressing in each ear. The correspondences of our flesh are too myriad to relate. Some, not translatable into words, are autonomic.

The silence of mirrors. Motions, shadows in mirrors making no sound. Not just the oval mirror in the front hall, but the dark interior mirror. The shadows mocked me. Your face was unaged, like an astronaut's, moving through memory time, not actual time, and it was also my face, drained of color, emptied of substance, the shape of the past. The future more tragic yet: dark days without even shadow.

What about now?

I want you and love you.

Now? This moment?

Yes.

I had to wait for him to finish his workday yesterday. By then I knew what I must do. I asked him to sit with me in the piano room/office and I asked him to listen with me to the tape of Theodora's last recital. He looked surprised, looked at my face, then he nodded. "OK."

I skipped the first part of the program and went to the Rachmaninoff. "The music sounds so far away," I whispered, surprised at the true air of the concert hall captured there, music recorded along with unavoidable rustles, coughs, and general background clutter on the tape. We filtered all that out as the tape proceeded.

"Was she that good?" I whispered.

"She was that good."

Her throat was producing notes which floated like fantastic balloons in the air, swelling or diminishing as she willed them. For the little space of the piece we were united with her again, going where she went, thinking her thoughts, feeling her passion. If it is true, as someone has said, that we possess no one except in memory, our memories summoned her to that live present. My throat was constricted, even as hers expanded. She sang the wordless notes of the *Vocalise* like they should be sung, without the artifice and polished cover-up that maturity brings to the diva.

Three-quarters through, John Mark was beginning to cry soundlessly. He took my hand as we sat on the worn leather couch under the shutters, about where the piano had been. He held tight to my hand and put his other hand over his face. I cried with him. She sounded like a child on a beach singing to waves, bestowing a last gift upon us. Then she left us. The song ended and the tape snapped off, rewindable but irreversible. After a few moments, he said, "It's over."

Today I awoke to peace. I also awoke feeling that Theo is dead. Whether in the body or in my mind, I do not know. I know that, wiping my breath from the oval mirror, I saw only myself. Then I saw a gold flash. I turned around. Sometime since the last time I looked—when was that? Yesterday, a lifetime ago?—he had put the pendulum back and the clock was in beat. My heart stirred into beat with it. The time on the face was correct.

Life is a trade-off. Perhaps she met someone. Perhaps we all gained more than we lost. Strechman and I have survived. Our marriage has survived. Over the years we have seen the body of our love change shape, deepen, twist, choke, starve, smolder, do everything but die. We gained more than we lost. Didn't we.

I will call the church for a Mass. "For Theodora." I will not say so, but I intend it for the final repose of her soul.

Desaparachos

The border checkpoint at Sarita was two days behind them now. They were walking north, thirteen people, in a loose double row on the single railroad bed. Every evening they materialized out of the brush and reassembled on the track like steel filings drawn to a bar magnet. The steel track was spiked to earth, glinted in the setting sun as far as the eye could see, and they clung to it tenaciously.

Occasionally they encountered mottes, or groves of scrub oak so thick that a man on horseback could not enter them. But coarse, tall grasses had managed to subjugate the oaks and everything else into open grazing land that shimmered in the August heat. The rail bed was built up to a height of fifteen feet, on a level with the tops of the mesquite. Mesquite and prickly pear each struggled with the tough grass to dominate this coastal plain that stretched out of sight in all directions. Between clumps of mesquite rolled an ocean of gamma grasses, blue stems, black-eyed Susans, Johnson grass, salt grass, and choke vine.

Lazario Fernandez watched for the plane, watched the turkey vultures. In El Salvador the vultures descended in flocks upon the body dumps. They circled here, too, black fingers on their wingtips, black fingers of death playing something slow on the air as on a silent instrument.

The people carried nothing now. Some of the men wore canteens on their shoulders or confiscated army flasks on their belts. Lazario did not even have a machete, just his shirt and pants, canteen, and leather sandals. They had been told to throw away their straw hats, which identified them immediately as aliens. He wished now that he had a hat of some kind. The few women in the group wore cotton dresses or cotton blouses and skirts, plastic or leather slides on their feet. Some wore babushkas over their heads, tied at the nape of the neck; some wore aprons. They might have been going out to feed the chickens, in that better time when there were chickens. The boy Tomasito, in ragged jeans and a T-shirt with a Coca-Cola logo on the front, moved around at ease in the group, at times up front, at times trailing to throw gray rocks from the rail bed, seldom with his mother, and usually with Lazario. Once he found a rusty spike, carried it for a while, then cast it away with a clang, against the railing. Once, with surprise in his voice, Lazario pointed out a sea gull to him.

Tomasito missed the friends he had left at the refugee camp in Honduras. Here on this road there was no one his age, just some much older boys. He missed Chucho, a wraithlike female dog he had called his dog, one that had haunted the camp for a few months before it died of starvation. There was a school at the camp and they had let him attend even though he was only five years old. The teacher, herself a *campesina*, drew things with chalk on an old painted door. She drew melons and squash, rows of corn, and the children counted, "*uno, dos...*" He liked the drawings the others made in the camp school. The big soldiers were always turned sideways shooting dotted lines at the fallen, falling, or standing little people whose arms were raised up. He wanted to draw these things also. He had seen these things and much more: helicopters dropping out of the sky and shooting through the village, and bombs falling, trucks of soldiers shooting guns, houses on fire. He had seen a woman with her mouth shot off. She was a stranger who had walked with his people from their village of Tenancingo with her mouth gone and just a big black and bloody O as if she was saying O. But he wouldn't draw this woman now if he had pencil and paper. He would draw planes and houses on fire.

He snapped his finger. "Chucho. Chucho. Come." He felt bad enough inside to cry. The rocks on the rail bed pressed hard through the soles of his sandals. So he stepped tie to tie on the track. As he stepped left and right he chanted in cadence "ronald-reagan, ronald-reagan."

Legs moving, mile after scorching mile, infinitesimally slow, the human train inched its way along the track in the sunset. Crouched far to the north, what was to be the 5050 run, a short haul, took shape in the Corpus Christi yard. Its truncated head end, a pair of snub-nosed diesels and thirteen cars of bauxite, automobiles, and reefers, or refrigerator cars, foregathered strength, inched backwards to reinforce itself with thirty cars of Portland cement destined for Matamoros. The brakeman hung on the lead car of the load they were picking up and hand-signaled the engineer, O. W. Sludd. Air brakes blasted the air, wheezed like an asthmatic giant. The body of the train shuddered along its length as the automatic couplers clashed and held fast. The brakeman climbed into the cab with Sludd and the conductor, Mack Partin. They were set to go.

Down the track the red stare of the signals. An incoming Mo-Pac freight from San Antonio lumbered through. Then they got the green light and slowly moved the 5,000-odd tons off the siding onto the mainline. Green on the overhead bridge signals. Green all the way down the track. The dispatcher moved them out at 7:39 P.M. and they eased past the yard limit at 7:45.

"Going to ball it now?" Mack Partin was well aware that the engineer was no talker. He took this fact, however, not as a deterrent, but a challenge. The older man gave Partin a blank look for an answer, leaned on the throttle. The engines, combining 3600 horsepower each and 250 tons of thrust back-to-back, accelerated smoothly. Partin waved from the left side of the cab to some early evening porch-sitters in Greasertown as the sun got off some final malevolent shots at the tan stucco shacks, turning them to dull mustard. Then he grinned at the brakeman sitting behind him, and settled back in his comfortable upholstered seat.

The boy's mother Rafaela caught up with him as he marched along on the ties. She wanted him with her before the sun went down. "Are you thirsty?" she asked.

"Yes."

She asked Lazario for water and he handed her the canteen. She opened it, held it to the boy's mouth, and took it away when she thought he was drinking too much. The group had brought several dozen corn tortillas from Matamoros in plastic bags. In the two days on this railroad track, they had eaten them all, rolled them up empty and eaten them. During the day they hid themselves in the chaparral and ate mesquite beans. The tiny immature beans were mild and nutty, but scarcely larger than sesame seeds.

Lazario scanned the skies constantly for the tiny dot of an airplane, listened for the sound of rotor blades slapping the air. There had not been a helicopter yet, but the plane circled low, like a great lazy buzzard, all day long. The plane would circle a three-mile radius twice every two hours. From their hiding places in the mesquite they could see the pilot's head on the turns.

There were many ground doves under the brush. He listened to the doves sounding the same two-note dirge, over and over. They were always in two's, doves. Such a sad mating call. Why are you sad? he thought. You have each other. And you are free. Hungry as he was, he would not have eaten a dove at this moment. I have been hungrier, he thought.

He was thirty years old, but looked like any age over forty. He could have been a Mayan stone figure: thick lips and a hawk nose, puffs under his eyes. But the face was gaunt, not round, and he had the beginnings of a widow's peak and a black beard. If he made it through Texas into the U.S. he must get a job to send money back to San Salvador, to his wife, children, and other family members, twelve in all. One of them was a boy Tomasito's age.

He said to Rafaela, "August 9. There will be moonrise by 10:30." He was silent for a long time while he worried. Would the coyote meet them as he said? They had paid $500 each to be trucked into the country from Matamoros. The coyote had dumped them north of Armstrong, Texas; he said he could not drive with them past the border patrol checkpoint. He was to pick them up again about fifty miles north at a point between Riviera and Ricardo. They would meet behind a deserted cafe called The Diner, he said. It was just north of Riviera. They calculated together that they should arrive at the cafe by dawn of the third day. To do this they had made seventeen miles a night on foot and must make seventeen more tonight. Lazario worried. The birds sounded their notes, like a woman crying in imperfect Spanish, Oh, nooo. Oh, nooo.

"I will be glad when it is dark," said Rafaela. "The night is our friend." They had started out well before dark today to make better time and because the country was uninhabited. Rafaela could not get accustomed to the openness of the land. She wanted to crouch and run, and she wished for thickly overgrown trails, fog-hooded volcanic slopes to press against, underground places in which to hide. They were making good progress, according to Lazario. There were no signs of human habitation, although day and night they could hear the not-so-distant waves of traffic on the highway. Once or twice they heard a cow bellow far away. There was the buzzing of insects in the chaparral and the cooing of doves. When their voices were very quiet one could hear every minute or so the track itself, like a living thing, crack or groan from the stress-shifting of the bed. Other than this there was no sound. There were only the dark green waves of mesquite on the sea of tall grasses; and the straight and endless track north.

"Tomasito." She put her hand on the boy's hair. It was as hot as if the coarse blue-black strands were tiny electric wires warming up. He tossed her hand away as she ruffled up his hair. He knew he was her world now and the thought oppressed him.

Rafaela thought of a village they had passed on their journey. The widows were walking out in a long line at dawn to plant the corn. The fear and anger that periodically possessed her body took hold of her again. She began to shake and cry.

"What's the matter?" Lazario pulled his attention away from the sky to the woman. His concern, fleeting as it was, opened up her emotions.

"Oh God! The men get their revenge. They take guns and machetes and hack the soldiers' bodies and booby-trap them. But where is our revenge? Mine and my child's?"

"What happened to your husband?"

"A bomb fell on our village," she sobbed. "I never saw sights like that in five years of war."

"It was in the daytime?"

"Yes, in broad daylight. Because there was no way we could fight back."

He was a city man, not a *campesino*, and he chanted a string of obscenities under his breath.

"Tomasito and I were spared because we had gone to haul water. We and a few others survived. I buried my husband under what was our house before." She cried and spoke brokenly, hardly taking a breath, releasing the memories of that day in a torrent of rapid Spanish. "Then I buried two women friends who had no one left to do it. All their body parts were together except Yolanda's. They were in the bomb crater, already in their graves." She laughed hysterically. "Tomas! Tomas! What have they done? Luz! Yolanda! Look what they've done! Who will plant the corn? Who? God! God!" She looked around wildly at the strange landscape, seemed not to know where she was. But she kept walking, moving her legs forward stiffly, and gradually she calmed down. He could give her nothing but a willing ear and his presence.

"All right, Rafaela, all right," he said. The setting sun bled through a ragged tear in the clouds. The patient buzzards swung slowly in a big circle.

The Silent One walked with them, pregnant, three steps behind her man. She was Pipil Indian, Lazario knew, even though she didn't dress that way. Pipil had lost their language and hidden their ways because they had been considered Communist even as far back as the massacre at Matanga in 1932. The woman—Lazario thought her name was Antonia—trudged along stupidly, in the Indian women's way, as dogs to whom their masters come or not, as they please. But something more had happened to her. Lazario knew this. The silence was not just stupidity and the Indian way.

He glanced to his right, to the widow Jesusa, wondering how he could turn her from a liability to an asset. Traveling alone, Jesusa slept badly during the day under the mesquite trees. The mesquite was fully leafed out. Its fringed, fernlike leaves gave good cover. They could not be seen from above if they huddled near the base of the trees.

"These cactus," Jesusa would grumble, pointing out the prickly pear all around them, "they like the shade, too. And what are these holes? Here and—here—and here—?" she asked sharply, pointing to the ominous holes with mounds of perfectly round dirt balls piled up around them.

"Snake holes," said Lazario.

"Ai-ee! Yi! ¡*Por Dios!*"

"You would rather be a *desaparacho*, then," Lazario said savagely.

She complained no more for the moment. The extreme heat, the constant tension, and the lack of sleep left her stiff every night with arthritis, and argumentative. She experienced heart pains and shortness of breath every night on the route. She was practically fearless, but she had a horror of snakes and scorpions, as did many of the others. In fact, she and some of the others had insisted on sleeping right there on the track, but Lazario had been adamant about that. Jesusa had also wanted everyone to kneel down on the track for a short prayer service each evening before they set out; just a prayer, a song, but Lazario had absolutely refused. If they wanted him to lead them out of there, they must do as he said and sleep in the sand under the mesquite. And time was too precious to spend in a prayer service. They must push ahead. Those who wanted to pray or sing softly could do so, as they walked. Otherwise let a woman lead them. Let Jesusa tell them what to do, or the Silent One. Only one could be the leader, and it had to be Lazario.

Jesusa was small, big-bosomed, hunch-backed, her long arms given to messianic gesticulations above the heavy crescent of her body, as if they were railing against its relentless return to the fetal position. She was very brown-skinned, with a face wrinkled like the map of a place with many streams and rivers. She was wrinkled far beyond her fifty-nine years. She had long straight black hair, parted in the middle, sometimes pulled back in a loose bun, sometimes hanging down her back. A big wooden crucifix hung on a leather string around her neck, identifying her as a Delegate of the Word, a prime target of the secret police. Like most of the others in the group, with the exception of a lone Mexican National, she had fled from Chalatenango Province, where the fighting was the most fierce, thence to a Honduran refugee camp.

She had abandoned a daughter, Anna Maria, a son-in-law, and seven grandchildren in what was left of Chalatenango because one memorable morning Anna Maria had heard a muffled noise, a thump on the front porch, and the roar of a vehicle leaving the scene. She had looked out with numb horror to see a Cherokee Chief pulling away from the house. Anna Maria opened the front door cautiously, then screamed and ran away. The naked body of her best friend, Felicitas, pushed the door the rest of the way and fell into the room. Felicitas had also been a Delegate of the Word. The body was covered with blood and the breasts had been hacked off. Jesusa fled the province the next day.

The sun was just gone down and Tomasito was tired already,

dragging his feet. "The night is our friend," Rafaela repeated to the boy. "It is safer at night." The Silent One kept pace with her. Lazario and Jesusa were walking with the Silent One's husband. "*Compa*," said Jesusa to the husband in the familiar. (She spoke to anyone, any time, any way she liked; hadn't she spoken at length to Archbishop Romero a week before he was killed?) "You have three strong sons with you. That is good."

"Yes," he answered. "We had others. I don't know how many. She knows."

There had been nine pregnancies before this one. The aide at the camp had patiently worked this information out of her, as with forceps. And with each "history," as she called it, it was as if Antonia was giving birth to that child again. Three children, the teen-aged boys with them, had survived. Two others, both girls, might have survived, but they were killed by government soldiers in a raid on village subversives. One baby had miscarried. Two had died of worms. One of diarrhea. ("Enteritis," wrote the aide.) These had died in the years that they made payments on their land. They lived in fear of losing their land. Antonia's uterus responded to the memory with pain. Every year it was the same: make the payment or keep the money for food. Finally, two bad seasons and a third season of war that turned Chalatenango into scorched earth had finished them. ("It is necessary," said the aide. "For proper care during your pregnancy, it is necessary to know how they died.")

Antonia let escape a little wail and continued to walk three steps behind her man, wailing. The man, embarrassed, reminded her that they must be quiet. He excused the woman. "She has nerves."

Rafaela put her arm around the woman's waist. "Now, *compa*," she said. "Now."

"*¡Cristo vive en la solidaridad!*"

Jesusa sang the last line of the verse in a cracked basso, over and over, that last line, to the rhythm of her walking. Lazario worried to the cacophony of her noise and the soft murmurings of the group and the sad love songs of the doves. If they reached the old empty cafe tomorrow morning and the coyote was not there, they would hide in the brush until dark. At dark they would walk until they reached a place where there was a church and ask the priest for mercy, for sanctuary.

"Lazario Fernandez, keep up your spirits. Sing!" ordered Jesusa.

"I will sing when I get out of Texas." He patted her hump. For luck. "Ask the good Christ for a safe passage," he said. "Ask Him to speak His Word to Salvador."

"Ask Him yourself."

"I got tired of waiting for the truth to descend. See! I said. The truth does not descend. It rises from below. It speaks out of the earth—the bloodsoaked earth."

"Ah! When you stumble in the dark, does not someone grab your arm? Has some friend or old uncle not always been there to give you counsel and strength? Who do you think that was, grabbing you and speaking to you?"

"I save myself. I counsel myself. I listen to no one."

"And Salvador is you!"

"Salvador is a man castrating himself. Salvador is a woman stabbing herself to death. Flesh wounds, insane, you see, deep flesh wounds. One of them will be to her guts one day soon. And then to the heart."

The arms thrust themselves at him like striking brown serpents. "Put all that out of your mind! Until we can do something about it. All we can do is pray. We are in another country."

"The smell of blood is here too. Don't you smell it? And you say, 'Come, let's forget all that now, let us forget!'" He jerked his hands up at her stiffly and then let them fall uselessly to his sides. "Ah, old woman. It's not your fault. Go on. Go. Leave me alone."

"What will you do then? Shout at the sky?"

"Leave me alone." He added, silently, "*¡Chingala!*"

A deep sense of futility filled his being. He knew suddenly that the coyote would not be there. Everything that they were doing would prove to be useless. Twelve people on his hands. So easy to spot. They would be captured. He had twelve of his own to think of, in San Salvador.

He would go on alone. He must go on alone. By the time the others missed him he would be gone.

He turned sharply away from the track and slid down the roadbed, as though to walk over to the nearest bush to relieve himself. He let the people get some distance ahead of him, then moved away from them in waist-high grass, but still toward the north.

He heard Tomasito call out for him once: "Lazario!" Then all was quiet. The silent expanse of grass without landmark, the open rangeland, was like a dreamscape, as if he was on the moon, and yet still looking up in the sky for the missing moon. He strode on.

A skinny pig trudged along a muddy alley in a village in his mind. That day had also been like a dream. He didn't remember which village it was, but the rib-racked pig was in the muddy thoroughfare between the huts, its ears drooping over its downcast eyes. He had a fever, so he had followed a nurse from the street into a house being used as a med center. A starved baby was dying there, pop-eyed, staring fixedly at nothing. His nine-month-old body, gray in the gray light, lay in a baby scale. The medic was trying to nudge the weight bar upward toward eight pounds. The little being had sparse dull black hair on its skull. A little old man's face. It was as though someone had squeezed an old man small and drained him of all his juices. He stared at nothing, knew nothing, a bony forefinger caught inside his bottom lip. His little breastplate of ribs looked molded onto him. And bones, bones for arms and legs, smaller bones for feet. Belly was the biggest part of him, its gray melon globe ending in a sturdy little circumsized stem, strangely vital and strong. But this, too, had given up, the little vine dried up during the night and died.

Tomasito. *¡Chingala!* He veered to his right, quickened his pace until the railroad track was in sight again, climbed to the rails, and trotted down the roadbed until he caught up with the people.

"When the poor believe in the poor, then we can sing freedom."

The old woman was still singing. Lazario fell back, took hold of Tomasito, who was lagging, and swept him up onto his shoulders. He grasped Tomasito's legs firmly, pinned them close to himself. The others were picking up Jesusa's song. "Ai! You!" He interrupted the singing. "Let's be quiet."

"We were singing very softly," they insisted.

When the poor announce to the poor
The hope that Christ gave us
Then the Kingdom is born among us.

He began to cry noiselessly. The moonless night seized him, the troubled dreaming of all the people in the lands they had crossed, all of them tossing under this unconcerned moonless sky. The danger of the coming day, his far-off family, the collective losses of these companions here, the bloodsoaked earth behind them, the smell of it following them, each seized him with its despair. His eyes brimmed, tears ran into his beard, overrunning his face with sorrows that seemed to have been seeping over centuries far back in the caves of his eyes.

"Stop singing," he told Jesusa. "Christ has been disappeared."

She stopped singing. "Oh, no! But Jesus is walking with us this moment! He suffers what we suffer!"

He wiped tears and sweat onto his sleeve. "All right, Jesusita, all right." He kept his eyes on the track.

"There is a railroad bridge ahead." The Mexican came to him with the word. Some of the people were already beginning to cross it.

"Wait," said Lazario.

"Shall we go down the bank, wade the creek, and go up the other side? How deep is the water? Come on, let's go across it."

"Wait." He silenced them. They could hear nothing. The

distance from the approach to the other end of the trestle
seemed to be about 450 feet. He peered down the track past the
trestle into the blackness. "There is nothing coming. Walk
carefully. There is no railing." With Tomasito still on his back he
watched until most of the others had set out across it. It was not
hard to cross. "It's like climbing a horizontal ladder," Jesusa
joked. "Just put your feet in the right places." Lazario walked
gingerly. He could not help but think of booby traps. There was
no clearance on either side, just a sheer drop into empty air.
There was a heavy smell of creosote. The others began to sing
again as a slight Gulf breeze revived their spirits.

Partin turned to the brakeman. "Open country ahead. No
stops! This is my kind of run. I just come off of Paisano Summit
in Presidio County. Talk about a pisser! A full two per cent
grade! A feller wouldn't believe Texas has that kind of mountain
road." He reached under the seat, pulled out a thermos, waved it
in the direction of the man behind him, but the brakeman had
his own coffee handy. Partin poured a cup and held it out to
Sludd, who shook his head without looking at him. Sludd wore a
green polyester jumpsuit and boots and a dark denim railroad
cap. His neck, the back of it, looked like it was quilted. He was
clean everywhere else. But it seemed like there was black down
in those creases back of his neck and that no washing would get
the grime out of there. His hair of no color, maybe dark yellow
that had turned three-quarters gray, scraggled down into some
of the creases.

Partin himself never wore anything but boots, jeans, and
Western shirts. He poured the coffee down, real Texas coffee
from Earline's Cafe—pale and burnt-tasting. He drained the
plastic cup with a sound like "Ahhrgh"—impossible to distin-
guish if it were relish or revulsion—and screwed the cup back on
the thermos. His eyes hazed over as he watched the control
panel in front of him. He thought of LaWanda. Thought of her
twice a day, dawn and sunset. The little box he had for her in his
pocket gave him a warm feeling. He tried again with Sludd. "I

picked up a little gewgaw for my wife...." He unsnapped the
pearly button on his shirt pocket and took the box out. "I bought
her a pire of earbobs in Corpus. See there? Sterling silver
oilwells. Think she'll cut a figure, one hanging in each ear?" The
engineer glanced at the earrings, gave an unsmiling nod. Stared
down the track again with his jaw jutted out. He's bitter as hell,
Partin thought. Bitter as them coffee dregs. He and the brakeman settled back to talk railroading.

The sun had set at 8:18. They had passed the Chapman
Ranch. They were now traversing the boundary of the King
Ranch. There was nothing but mile after mile of fenced prairie.
Kingsville lay ahead, but it was not a scheduled stop. They were
routed straight through to Brownsville. The engineer switched
on the twin sealed beams that lighted their way through Kingsville, and after Kingsville, the coastal prairie again. They roared
on through a little fly-by place named Ricardo, and another by
the name of Riviera. At Riviera, the engineer cut the speed
some and seemed to relax, but only a tad. He leaned back in his
padded armchair, took a toothpick from his chest pocket,
worked on his brown teeth.

"What'd you say your wife's name was?"

"LaWanda. I got two kids at home, a girl and a boy. Older
boy's in the Navy." Something prevented him from asking Sludd
anything personal.

He wondered why they were slowing down from fifty-five to
fifty. Then he remembered the Olmos Creek trestle. They were
beginning to cruise the long leisurely curve flanked by dense
trees and underbrush that uncoiled onto the trestle over Los
Olmos Creek. The other couple of times Partin had run this
route, the engineer had started sounding the signal here, even
well before the point they were now passing. Although neither a
signal nor a reduction of speed was required by regulations, the
other engineers gave it the signal here: O___ . Short and long,
short and long. The thought stabbed him, made him sit up
uneasily, nervously: an engineer had told him wetbacks had
been killed on this trestle before.

"Ain't you going to signal for Olmos Creek?"

"Nope."

"You ain't going to signal for the trestle?"

"If a son of a bitch is that sorry he sets foot on a trestle, it's his lookout."

"But they say there's been wetbacks killed on it."

"Sure enough?"

"Man, the curve and the brush block the view! You ought to tie that whistle down right now!" He was on his feet, clenching his hands together, trying to keep them off the signal pull. "Ain't you never hit nobody on the trestle?"

"I never been notified I hit nobody. I strictly follow regulations, buddy." He turned his face toward Partin. His jaw stuck out angrily with the toothpick still hanging out of it, and his one visible eye under the railroad cap crackled and flashed like a match under the thumbnail: "You better lay off."

Partin stared. He gaped at the set jaw and the puckered and creased nape of Sludd's neck. It was the last thing he saw before the engine pounded onto the trestle and they both saw the people in the net of the headlights.

The apprehension of the train struck every heart at the same time. They felt slight trembling under their feet. Almost simultaneously they all heard the awful rhythm of the engine and saw the light. The light did not turn directly on them at first. Then it turned directly on them and then the scream of the whistle began, and the screech of brakes and the horrible gnashing of wheels against steel track mingled with the screams of the people. All this burst upon them as from the gates of hell, and they called upon God, mother, father, to help them as they turned and ran, stood momentarily paralyzed, or jumped into the shallow creek thirty-one feet below. Most were aware that they were beyond the point of no return, and these jumped into blackness, but two or three, including Lazario, at the trailing edge of the group, turned and ran. Jesusa, transfixed by pain, stood in the spread brilliance of the light. In the face of this confrontation her heart had convulsed. It gave up beating, she fell, and she was dead before she hit the water.

Rafaela turned to look for Tomasito and saw him above the crowd, bouncing on Lazario's back as they scrambled away; then she jumped.

The train pursued them, blaring its useless warning. The wooden foundation shook under Lazario's feet. Screams tore at him from behind. He had thought at first he could make it back; now dread and horror engulfed him, his legs were jelly. He concentrated on the inspired game plan that had come to him when the light had first netted him: to turn and run, never looking back, stepping, not broadly so as to risk stumbling, but to take smaller steps at a tremendous speed, smaller steps on every other tie; that was it, skip a tie, skip a tie, set up a breakneck rhythm. It was a dance for life.

He felt something striking at his back. It was his canteen. Everything was bathed in light. He could see quite well where he was, and he managed to regain the south bank. He leapt off the trestle as the train crashed by with its brakes shrieking. He and Tomasito fell several feet onto the slope of loose rocks under the trestle. The child was thrown from his shoulders as they rolled and slid in the rocks, but before Lazario even got to his knees he could hear with profound relief Tomasito's involuntary healthy wails for his mother. He found the boy and hugged him close. "Mama! Mama! Mama!" the boy screamed, out of his head, bleeding from cuts on his face and arms. Lazario's knees and hands felt like they were cut to ribbons. There was no one around where they were, but he could hear shouting below.

He carried the boy piggyback again, descending the slope with Tomasito screaming in his ears. In the semidarkness he could see a scattered group of people clawing their way up the opposite bank, making for open country.

Now he began to hear under Tomasito's sobbing, under the panting of the stalled train, and the intermittent idiotic squalling of its whistle, some moans and soft cries on the banks of the creek. By their voices he found two compatriots, still alive, too injured to move. One was the Mexican National. One was a Salvadoran woman. "Lie and wait," he said to the injured. "They will send an ambulance." He gave them a little water from his canteen. Rafaela must be dead, he thought. She would not run away until she found Tomasito. She might be hiding in the bushes. He called to each clump of bushes he came to, "*Compa...Compa...*Rafaela! Rafaela! Jesusa! Jesusita!"

Suddenly he ducked aside and flattened himself against a concrete pedestal. Two *Norteamericanos* were coming, sliding down the embankment, calling something unintelligible. Lazario lunged away from them. He waded quickly through the water with Tomasito, splashing his own face and reaching behind to dab the child's face with the water to try to quiet him.

The water was three or four feet deep at midpoint. He saw no one in the water or on the other side of the creek. They were either dead on the bottom or they had crawled out into the brush, injured, or had escaped. He fervently hoped that there were no dead ones, but recalling now the screams behind him on the track, he feared that some had been plowed under and dragged or thrown to their deaths.

Fear carried him to the base of the opposite bank and commanded his legs to move him and his burden up the steep slope. His hands grew tendrils that attached to anything, grasped at everything. He jammed his feet, knees, elbows into inappropriate crevices to keep from sliding back down. He finally scrambled up the bank, reached level ground, and did not stop to catch his breath, plunged on in a generally northern direction but not along the track.

"Hey, you, stop!" one of the trainmen called. The other echoed, "Stop and help!"

He did not see another living soul. Those who had climbed the bank had scattered and were gone, or were in hiding. Only when he got about a hundred yards away and climbed a little rise, did he stop and turn around. He disentangled his canteen, opened it, and lifted it over his shoulder to the boy. Then he drank.

I let them be trapped! I am responsible for those who died. But where did it come from, that train? *Señor*, you are my witness, we neither saw nor heard the train! The train did not signal until it saw us!

"The ambulance will come," he said to the boy. "The ambulance will take her to the hospital."

It had been necessary for the train to back up two miles from its final stopping place. It lay inert now, distant, black, sprawled halfway across the trestle. The tail trailed off into darkness, the head illuminated the complex webwork, its great eye surveying the night's work.

He looked up to the sky. He had never seen the night sky open like this, immense. Stars. Stars flung everywhere. Still no moon, and the vast sky a much darker vault now, unfathomable.

He was trembling. Well, *Señor*, I am lost. I have no map of the way I am to go.

He sank unsteadily in the weeds with the boy on his back. On his knees, he crossed himself as deliberately as if he were taking the measure of himself. *"En el Nombre del Padre, el Hijo, y el Spiritu Santo."* Then he got up slowly, placing his bleeding hands on the earth to support the weight of himself and the boy. It was a struggle to get himself erect again. When he had done this, he tightened his throbbing hands into fists, held them out to the south. "And in the name of man!" In blessing, in malediction, he shouted it: *"¡En el nombre del hombre!"*

The boy had not spoken since he stopped crying. "I will walk now," he said. Lazario put him down and turned the boy's shoulders around. They moved on. Soon they disappeared.

A Certain Lot or Parcel of Land

Le Petit Déjeuner

The lime-green chameleon was lord of the bush on which he perched. His skin was fresh and green as new leaves, skin that fitted closely over tiny ribs the size and brittleness of raw vermicelli. He leapt to the window above him and flicked his way up the shutter, punctuating his run with sudden stops, at which time he raised and lowered his head in minute mechanical increments to survey his domain. As if he didn't know he was the very last of his species in Harmony, again he raised his regal head, this time especially high, and thrust out his brilliant red ruff in courtship display to a nonexistent female.

He was crawling over appliqués of blue-gray and rust colored lichen that clung tight to the dead unpainted wood, bringing it back to life with a patina, a textured blending of soft, exquisite colors possible only after many years of neglect.

Their houses had never known paint, but they had been kept in repair, the yards and fences kept up. Now all the houses around them were quickly growing up in weeds. The weeds spread right up to the chain-link fence where, just on the other side, they turned into green lawn and white gravelled roads named after the chemicals produced there: Vinyl Lane, PVC Boulevard, Chloride Road.

Unnatural. That was Niobe's estimation of the whole thing when she was thinking most clearly, as now, waking from fitful sleep. The rotten egg smell, the white powder everywhere, the roar of the plant to where you could not hear birds sing. The towering flares that burned all day and made the night day, too. At sunset all the plant was lit up like a monster Christmas tree. Unnatural, to see the lanes empty, the front gates opening on one hinge to shells of hip-roofed row houses. To see clotheslines, long ago stripped of their wet wash, sagging and corroded.

She sighed before she opened her eyes. She had a headache and faint queasiness. "It ain't the smell making me sick today," she thought, "it's the Dedication and the Reception." The dedication of Harmony Estates would be taking place this morning, followed by a brunch and reception at the Mayor's house in Plancher-des-Vaches. Plancher-des-Vaches was the hub, and Harmony and a half a dozen other Negro communities were the outermost spokes. Niobe was going to be at the reception, but as kitchen help lent by Miss Claudine for the occasion to Miss Solange, the Mayor's wife. Niobe sighed again and forced her eyes open to the morning.

In the other bedroom Yolanda stirred. Her eyelids sprang open. Droplets of sweat glittered above her lips, in her hairline, and on the tips of her wiry tendrils of hair. She was fifteen, but still, like a child, sweating in the head. Her dream was still wrapped cozily around her: of a brick house that had a brand new refrigerator and air conditioning! It had screens and windows that went up and down. No more shutters. It had wall-to-wall soft carpets that were like walking ankle-deep in clouds.

She got out of bed and went to the open window, banishing the lizard from sill to shutter again, where he eyed her coldly from a safe distance. She hadn't seen a lizard for a long time. In these lanes where she grew up, girls chanted, "Liz-zard, liz-zard, show me your blank-ket." The bushes and vines used to be full of them. If one of them paid you mind and showed his blanket, which was a red stiff piece of skin that came out under his throat, it was because he was going to make out with a female. God help you if you picked him off a bush when he was showing his blanket. He could bite the hell out of your finger and he would not let go. She smiled and thought of her boyfriend A.J. "Hey, Yo, look at this!" And he would be dangling five lizards out in front of her, one clamped down on each finger. Sometimes A.J. would put one to sleep by holding its little hard-breathing sides and gently stroking its belly. He'd lay it down in the grass and it would stay like that for quite a spell with its four little claws sticking straight up.

Quick as a wink, this one turned from green to brown and jumped away, twisting down the rough gray boards of the house, leaving pinprick footprints and long drag marks from his tail in the fine white dust on the window sill.

They were almost all gone, but she didn't miss them. She was sort of scared of them. Maybe her grandmother was right. "Everything goin'." There sure was no more river shrimp, her grandmother repeated like a broken record. Yolanda had never seen river shrimp. They were among the first to go. "Now you don't see no more mosquito hawks, lightning bugs—"

"They must of been pretty," said Yolanda.

"—no more green moss, not even a buzzard on the highway anymore. Lemme tell you, Yolanda—"

"Yo."

"—when ol' buzzard can't breathe the air, it's time to get out."

"Then, Grandma, we got to get out. Don't you see that?"

"You think I am gon' move into that mess of porridge?"

"Why do you always call it that?"

"It's in the Bible. Read your Bible."

"It's not my Bible."

"Hesh! Hesh your mouth, Yolanda."

"Yo. Grandma, I'm sorry. You just make me so mad with your obstinacious ways!"

Yolanda closed her shutters against the roar of the plant and the view of the next-door yard where a rusted-out truck cab was bedded down in the weeds without its chassis. In the tiny tacked-on bathroom off the kitchen, she got ready for her workday at Burger King. As she flushed the wheezing toilet, she paused to rap her knuckles hard against the tank to indicate to herself the precise hardness of her grandmother's head.

They had only coffee for breakfast. They had not been cooking much. They didn't tend the garden. Everything, the earth, the rain, the air they breathed, seemed already to belong to Gulf Atlantic. Her grandmother just would not give it up.

They took up the thread of argument again.

"Move to a don't-care neighborhood. Humph!" said Niobe, placing a milk carton in the refrigerator and automatically kneeing the door firmly in place to make it stay.

Yolanda sighed like an eighty-year-old woman. "Yeah, we gon' rot here."

"My head unbowed. Long as Greater Mt. Sinai still here and people come back here to church on Sunday, I stay here."

"Grandma, you know that won't last forever."

"Mt. Sinai the first and last thing here. We been here 99 years. I saw the copy of the deed at the church, talking about arpents and feet and inches, yes, precious inches of land we bought from Grenoble. Bounded by the river, it said, bounded by Bayou Triste. It was signed by the preacher and the deacons. We were freedmen then, you know. The freedmen bought the land from the Vaucoudrais on Grenoble, and then the church sold the lots to the congregation, you see. We come together in the name of the Lord all the way back then, you see. Pretty soon, along come a storm, the 1909 storm, took the church down. It was wood, setting on bricks. Brother Edwards was a carpenter and he put it up again for $120. My grandaddy and every male assessed $5. My grandmother and every female assessed $3. Because the fieldhands made two bits a day more than the kitchen help."

Yolanda listened politely and sipped her coffee.

"When they built the new levee we had to move—just pick up and move when they say move, to what was old Bonne Heure. Some tore they house down and used the boards to build them again on Bonne Heure. My daddy and some others rolled they houses here—this here house, you see—drug by mules drawing the cables round a capstan."

Yolanda got up, rolled up the bag of coffee on the counter.

"The ladies in Harmony taught school in that church before we had schools. Sometime along there, after the war, we got electricity, and buses to come take the children to colored schools in Plancher-des-Vaches."

"Grandma, I have to get to work."

"Don't worry, I'm gon' carry you over there when I go to the Mayor Reception. I'll be ready when you are. Don't take me no time to get ready. I just need me a clean handkerchief for my hair. Get me one from the draw, Yolanda." She followed her granddaughter to the chifforobe in her bedroom. "Do you know, we lost that church again from Hurricane Betsy! All this before you ever born. And built it again!"

"Yeah, thass something."

"And your mother baptized in the river right over there." She pointed the opposite way. "Buried over there. My daddy, mother there, and your other grandparents. Your aunts and uncles there, and my two nieces. I paid up with the Laboring Sisters and I be there too, directly."

Yolanda wished she wouldn't talk like that. She put the bag of coffee in the refrigerator and did a bump and grind against the door.

"We had everything we need. Little tomato and bell pepper garden here, catfish in the barrow pits by the river—" Niobe gestured with elegant long fingers beyond the window, where whitewashed concrete-over-brick sepulchers sat next to simple wooden roundtop boards that served as markers. "—graveyard over there right up next to the Gulf Atlantic fence. We paid our burial insurance, $3 a year to the Laboring Men Benevolent Association in the church, and the L.M.B.A. took care of us. We had our say-so in that church and in our family. Nobody telling us what to do."

"Yeah."

"That what made us stick together so, in good time and bad."

"Then how come so many left out of here so fast?"

"We didn't hold together like I was hoping. We really broke up."

"A.J. moved to Harmony Estates. Etheline, and Devon Grange family, and the Mitchells, they took they money and moved to New Orleans, Baton Rouge, Texas. Sima say—"

"Sima! Sima people so scared Gulf Atlantic gon' change they mind, Sima people left with they coats flapping on they behind!"

Yolanda couldn't help laughing at the picture.

"Yeah, laugh. My head unbowed."

Le Déjeuner

The automobiles parked in front of and around the side of the classic Greek Revival home reflected the part of town from which they had been driven this morning. The Gulf Atlantic top management and their wives—Solange Vaucoudrais' milieu— were represented by a full palette of luxury motor cars— Cadillacs, Lincolns, and Chryslers in Manet pinks, blues, and creams. Other Cadillacs, old and fish-tailed, and sparkling clean, were driven by the black minister, Reverend Battiste, and a few more prosperous members of his congregation. Niobe's old, low-slung Mercury was parked around the back.

The black families alighted from the automobiles together, descended on the Mayor's house together, and clung together like a swarm of bees, moving from room to room as one unit. Some of them brought children and grandchildren for a one- chance peek at high living from the vantage point of sitting room instead of kitchen.

Father Blouin of St. Michael-St. Gabriel came late in the clerical gray Detroit sedan, stripped, to which he had consigned

himself until he made Monsignor, an imminent prospect. He
had seldom been to the Vaucoudrais home. Business or social or
spiritual contacts with the family were made at City Hall or at
civic functions such as this, or in the confessional box. In this
sense he knew the most outward and the most inward of their
psyches, but nothing of the middle ground, in which world they
dwelt most of the time.

Solange was meeting all comers at the door. Father Blouin
noted that her black hair, this morning, was upswept into a kind
of cow pie atop her head. She was in a white linen sundress with
black patent accessories and onyx drop earrings. Her aroma was
strong, sweet, gracious, and invigorating, like her coffee.

"Solange."

They clasped hands and kissed each other's cheeks briefly.

"I'm sorry I'm late." He winced guiltily. "I had to bless an oil
well."

The craziness of their church, the craziness that the world
forced upon it, hit them both at the same time, and they laughed,
almost out of control.

"Really, I couldn't refuse this lady. She has been one of our
biggest supporters.

"Lulu Michaud?"

"Lulu Michaud."

"Why not?" Solange laughed again, making everything right.
She continued with some light talk that he scarcely heard. He
was looking beyond her tall figure to the heads of men and
women bobbing in the foyer and in the rooms to the side and
rear of the foyer. Strange to see black and white heads together
this way. A trickle of sweat started behind his ear and ran down
his jawline. Another trickle beaded on the tip of his curly
sideburn, peaked, trembled, and was pushed down his cheek by
still another budding bead. His usually pallid face was flushed
from the heat and the asininity of standing in ceremony in his
black suit and stole among half a dozen hardhats and the oil
heiress, Miss Lulu.

"Well, go on in, Father, and get a drink." He realized he had been just standing there, letting her talk. He had not made a move to go inside. The poor woman was exasperated with him, she was dismissing him. He walked into the first, the largest and most beautiful, of the three sitting rooms of the old mansion which Vaucoudrais had bought and renovated years ago. In this room a trio—piano, violin, and cello—was playing, with vigor, the Beethoven Archduke Concerto.

He took a martini from a tray of either-ors—martinis or Manhattans—offered him by a black waiter. He noticed the waiter had few customers among the black people. They were all watching each other. Some of them took a little glass of wine from another waiter. Solange must have decided that her usual champagne was too chi-chi for this gathering.

At the far end of the room the musicians' modest black feet tapped or turned lightly on a huge Tabriz carpet that seemed transformed from an autumn forest somewhere in the Caucasians, to a design in the head of a rare genius, to the magic in a dozen sets of fingers, to, finally, its unfurling on this unlikely floor in all its Euclidean glory. "A thoroughly fascinating thing," he thought, "upon which I might spend the entire morning meditating: I say 'upon which,'" Father Blouin said to himself in his homilitical manner (he often preached to himself)—"I say 'upon which' in its literal sense, because nothing would be more alluring than to kneel at its center, let the divine design flow into oneself, then mentally work one's way out of it again." Tempting though that might be, he must return to the party, to the dozens of white women's spike heels and black women's flats crossing, recrossing, and standing on the flung-out beauty.

A very large black woman in blinding white impassively held up a tray of hors d'oeuvres in front of him. He looked the tray over quickly and picked up a pink rosette-shaped something on a cracker. The maid, borrowed for the occasion from Claudine Paillot, moved heavily on about the edges of the room. Her feet were crammed into shoes from an orthopedic store in Baton

Rouge, which, while custom-cobbled for her employer's unique podiatric problems, could not and did not answer her maid's needs. What were sensible shoes for Claudine Paillot made no sense at all on Niobe's feet. Her bunions bulged out at various places on the shoes to give them an entirely new and grotesque shape. Under their heavy cargo, the shoes listed to leeward and starboard as she walked, like black boats about to capsize.

Niobe would not set foot on the rug, but somehow managed to serve the crowd from the fringes of the room. The rug was to be avoided at all costs, for at the center of it was nothing less than the black Evil Eye itself.

"All right, lemme speak to the Father here," came a hearty voice across the Caucasian Mountain borders of the rug.

"Reverend Battiste. Nice to see you." He and the Reverend Battiste shook hands.

"Does all this sound a lot to you like the Final Solution for the Jews? The 'Relocation,' I mean?"

"Not really," said Father Blouin coolly.

"Well, it's sad, but life the way we knew it is gone. Gulf Atlantic's emissions lowered our property values to zero. Then we began experiencing all these health problems. They had us squeezed up against the plant noise, the smells, and the flares one way and the river the other."

"That's true. But the company made a very generous offer to buy your property."

"Yeah, they come along and say, 'We are going to do this wonderful thing for your community and give you a brand new, modern suburb. We are going to improve the quality of your lives.'"

"I don't see it as all bad," said Father Blouin.

"Well, it's some good to it, I admit. But it sure reminds me of the Final Solution. They relocate you but they continue to poison the whole area to death. If we were the only ones it would be bad enough, but look at Morrisonville and Reveilletown, Good Hope, and Sunrise, all bought out, too. See, they want to be able to dump their poisons without complaints. They tell you when and where to go. It's the same old slave whip, Father Blouin. Different mens holding it."

Solange passed them and was tagged in desperation by Father Blouin. "Solange, tell us something about Grenoble. Didn't Harvey's family own it from the beginning?"

"No," she said. "The Vaucoudrais bought it from the Randolphs. The famous Virginia Randolphs. Same family. I don't like to bore people with all this family history, but Father, I know you're an amateur historian of this area. You see, Harvey's family has had it since the Civil War. And after the war it was Harvey's family that sold some of the land to the church to start the community of Old Harmony. Did you know that, Reverend Battiste?"

"Oh, yes, I am very aware of that."

"The people each had their own little plot and sharecropped for the plantation. Of course, most of the plantation land is sold off into subdivisions now. Mrs. Vaucoudrais still lives on Grenoble, you know. The family lost one house to the river and had to build again. Even this place—why, when Harvey and I bought this place, it had already been set back once from the river. And now it backs right onto the river again. Just a block away. Lord, we have to accept change, don't we?"

"Yes, we do," said Reverend Battiste. "Now I hear the Plancher-des-Vaches aquifer is threatened."

A pained look crossed Solange's face. She held out a hand as if fending off something, and turned away. "I'll be back in a little bit," she said hurriedly. "Have to see about something."

Niobe had been offering stuffed shrimp nearby and now she stood where the music of the trio drowned out everything. "Your house turn coming," she muttered to Solange's buttocks smartly revolving away from her. "Don't matter wherever you live. All turn to ashes, the Bible say. And Honey, all them ashes black. Black."

Solange's mission had evidently been to gather the company

for brunch, for she came back through the big rooms tolling a little gold bell, telling everyone to gather on the patio at the back. Blouin saw Harvey Vaucoudrais descending heavily down the stairs, as if reluctant to join the others until the last minute. From the way he looked, the priest thought it would not be surprising to find the Mayor himself a cancer statistic before too long. They shook hands and Harvey seemed genuinely glad to see him, clapped him on the back. They went out to the patio-garden area with the others. A kind of forced reverse discrimination was taking place. Everyone was deferring to the people of color, urging them to the head of the food line. Niobe now stood behind a chafing dish at a serving table, her face pulled down into an indelible scowl.

For Sissy Crocker, wife of the executive officer at Gulf Atlantic, and for Solange's personal friends and Service Leaguers, the menu held no surprises. Solange's best friend Claudine lifted hefty but highly selective servings onto her plate. "Sissy, take some of those baked truffled eggs. Mimi had them at Betsy's graduation breakfast and they are delicious." She moved on. "Mmmm, lobster Newburg. And stuffed mushrooms."

Claudine held out her plate to Niobe. "Thank you, Niobe. How are you today? But you know, Sissy, this is not so fancy compared to Solange's New Year's Day Dinner. Remember? Oysters Rockefeller. *And* Bienville. Caviar canapes. Remember the Baked Alaska with the love birds kissing each other on top? Remember her dove and duck dinner? Roast dove and pressed duck!"

Father Blouin chose the truffled eggs, Swedish meatballs, and tossed green salad. None of the ladies seemed overly impressed with the menu, he noticed. Many of these black ladies also doubled as someone's maid. They ate very high at times. When it came to food, he thought, the humblest white or black citizen knew how to eat like a king—at little cost.

Solange was using place cards, so the reverse discrimination was doomed to defeat. Her seating arrangement had been carefully thought out for optimum integration, not only of races, but of religions. She had been wickedly ruthless. Father Blouin found himself between a stout Greater Mt. Sinai deaconess and Sissy Crocker.

When all the guests were seated, an invocation seemed to be in order. The Mayor called upon Reverend Battiste, who set an innocuous, cautious tone. The food, as it has a way of doing, loosened everyone up. Father Blouin looked left. The deaconess was stolidly chewing. He looked right, to Sissy. She, too, was filling her tiny mouth. She also had a tiny nose, he noted, a too-cute nose—like a pet turtle, one of those painted ones. When she was not chewing, her tiny mouth was fixed in a slight pout. When she sat in the church on Sunday, it was no doubt a pious pout. At bedtime, a sexy pout, probably. She returned his glance.

"Faaaa-thah! I am so glad to sit next to you. Isn't this a wonderful occasion? All we have worked for so long is finally here. It really did my heart good to drive through Harmony Estates this morning and see what gumption and cooperation can do for a community. Charles said from the beginning he was going to spare no expense, pull out all the stops, for these people. I worked one day a week as a volunteer at the new Community Center myself and counseled people wanting more information. We had a huge undertaking there, Father, I assure you: talking with real estate agents, lawyers, and banks; locating schools, churches, and grocery stores near the home sites; contracting builders, and a hundred other things to make everything go smoothly. Charles says it was state of the art relocation. All the corporations are copying it. It is a showcase, Father." She glanced pointedly across the tables to her husband, who raised his arm in recognition, flashing a pair of cufflinks that seemed to Father Blouin like brightly buffed old gold Roman coins. From the distance he could not make them out. He would like to examine them closely later on. On the other side of Sissy Crocker sat the man in charge of the whole project, the company man from New York, who'd been sent down to facilitate the move. He was a black.

"Do you know," Sissy was saying, "Charles won't tell me the price tag on this, but it's rumored to be more than ten million. So many things factored in, like preserving the cemetery in perpetuity. Some of the people with more than one piece of property got hundreds of thousands of dollars. The minimum offered to anyone, even families in shotgun houses, was fifty thousand dollars."

"My."

"So we do feel we have improved the quality of life for everyone there. Of course, the church has to make a decision yet, and I understand there is one other holdout, an older lady, but I expect she will come around by the time the rest of the town is razed."

"When will that be?"

"By the end of the year. And speaking of that, Solange and I are cooking up a big surprise for Plancher-des-Vaches at Christmas."

"Really? What is it?"

"Oh, I can't tell you, or it wouldn't be a surprise. But it has to do with Old Harmony and Christmas." She, like others in town, was already calling it Old Harmony. She put her finger to her tiny lips. "Can't tell."

Solange was ringing her little bell again. When she got silence, she gave a little welcoming speech ("This will be short. You've heard enough speeches this morning"). Mayor Vaucoudrais was slightly under the weather today and he had recently passed the dedication festivities on to her, which she was delighted to undertake and she was thrilled to be a part of history in the making in Plancher-des-Vaches. She briefly told them some fascinating details ("facts unknown to whites"), about the community of Old Harmony, and mentioned that her personal interest was due to the fact that Harvey's family ("this *is* common knowledge") owned Grenoble, which sold the original land to the community. "But today our thoughts turn to the future and the safety and happiness we have secured for our black citizens and their children that we hold so dear, and

who are the future of Plancher-des-Vaches and the future of
the black race as well." She closed with a plea for cooperation
and goodwill from all the people of their city.

After her speech Father Blouin and Sissy Crocker turned to
the subject of travel in Europe, one of his passions. He was well
versed in European history and, especially, its art masterpieces.
As Sissy went on about good, bad, and execrable hotels, he
thought supercilliously, "When Charles takes you to Europe, it's
like taking a sandwich to a banquet." Among a local Catholic
clergy whose second home was Europe, he alone had never been
abroad. Neither he nor his family could afford it. Now he had a
patronness, the oil heiress, Mrs. Lulu Michaud, to send him. She
was very old and rich. She was an arch-segregationist. She was a
fiery anti-environmentalist.

Father Blouin thought Solange's speech was nicely spoken.
Did it fall on deaf ears? he wondered. He looked around. If not
on deaf ears, certainly on dumb mouths. The air that had been
buzzing with chatter just moments before was now deadly quiet.

Claudine was exasperated. Certainly it was so unfair of Solange
to jam them all together like this, Claudine thought, and then to
say, "Make small talk." Really, Solange, what did you expect? She
turned to her frail, nervous black neighbor. Where did one start?
"Darlin'," she asked, "do you have problem nails? I do."

Gradually, the conversation picked up again. There was even
some restrained laughter drifting from table to table. The guests
were being served brandied black cherries on vanilla ice cream,
Irish creme liqueur, and a demitasse. Solange let them linger as
long as it seemed serendipitous to do so. She was satisfied.
Things had gone pretty well, she thought. Presently she rose
again and called for Father Blouin to give the benediction.

"Instead of a prayer," he suggested, "why don't we all join
hands and sing 'Amazing Grace'?"

They held hands with awkward alacrity. Black-white. Black-
white. The strong mellow Negro voices led it off and the white
ones, higher pitched and sweetly melodic, joined in. Sissy

Crocker cried buckets during the song. She could not sing through to the end. Niobe did not hold hands. Neither did she sing. Neither did she cry.

As the members of the houseparty walked back through the house from the patio, their talk and laughter and the tinkling of chandeliers at times overpowered the trio which, after partaking of the stultifying lunch, had taken up its instruments again in the parlor. At times the music came back strongly and diffused its own dominant elegance throughout the rooms. Blouin was reluctant to leave. "What fabulous taste!" he exclaimed to himself. The post-luncheon Irish creme had made him feel fine. He had an urge to see the upstairs. Turning quickly at the base of the stairs, he took the steps two at a time. The bedrooms were less than breathtaking. They were utilitarian: beds like ancient battleships (had they been the scene of many an ancient battle?); cavernous bathrooms in which the massive fixtures stood like white limestone formations growing out of the marble floor.

He ducked into one of the bathrooms and came flat up against the Reverend Battiste, peeing. "Oops! Sorry!" He backed out again, traded places with Battiste when the Reverend came out. After he himself had finished, he washed his hands at a lavatory worthy of a Roman bath, and went out. There was Reverend Battiste, waiting for him.

"I didn't get to give you some figures downstairs," said Battiste. "You probably have heard or read these, but maybe not, they tend to suppress that information around here. Anyway, did you know that Gulf Atlantic P.-D.-V. Division put down 3.3 million pounds of toxins—"

"I know, I know. It's terrible."

"—*this* year."

"This year?"

"Every year, Father Blouin. Going directly into the air, the river, and the good earth. They tell me now the aquifer is threatened. Do you know there are 45 petro-chemical companies that dump in this parish?"

"Isn't that unbelievable?"

"We better believe it, Father Blouin. How many cancer victims you buried lately?"

"We sure come out looking bad on that."

"Our rates are among the highest in the nation for ten different kinds of cancer."

Blouin wished that this preacher didn't know so much. Or at least, didn't talk so much. It took away from the glow, the ambience he so seldom got to experience. Besides that, he had the Reverend's number. "When is your church moving, Reverend Battiste?"

"We continue to have services at the old site. The people come from everywhere. They are like those people who want to keep returning to the scene of a disaster."

"I heard that your congregation voted to leave the church where it is and continue to have services there, instead of letting Gulf Atlantic build a new one in Harmony Estates. The graveyard is there and they want the church to stay there. I also heard that you did everything in your power to get it razed and rebuilt in Harmony Estates. A brand new brick, debt-free church, eh Reverend? I can't say I blame you."

Another oriental, a red Bokhara runner, beckoned him down the hall. He excused himself. The hall was hung with a few family pictures and old steel engravings of obscure European spas. A few small fine occasional pieces also lined this hall. The red Bokhara was a real quality piece also. He flipped up a corner to check the sharp definition of the reverse pattern.

Downstairs, in the kitchen, Niobe set down the burnished copper chafing dish on a counter with a decided thud and walked out. "It ain't Harmony no more. Harmony belong to the dead in the graveyard." She was looking for the facilitator, the black company man from New York. She found him in the parlor, listening to the final strains of some musical composition. When she walked up to him, he said with a big smile, "Why hello, Mrs. James. I didn't see you at the dedication."

She looked him over. He did not have a face you would remember. The hand that held a drink of liquor had mother-of-pearl cufflinks where his hand went up his sleeve. "I wuddent there," she said.

"Mrs. James, I'm in my office in the Estates six days a week. I'd still be glad to talk to you, as long as I am still in town, any time, any day." His voice had a slightly teasing quality to it.

"What is the top dollar you paid for a house?"

"For a home in Old Harmony? We paid every single property owner at least $50,000, no matter what kind of house he lived in. Top dollar was, I believe, about $80,000."

"I will sell for $100,000."

His eyebrows went up. "I think we can negotiate that. Will you deal with me?"

"I just as soon deal with a canebrake rattler. What do you mean you can negotiate that?"

"I mean we can pay $100,000, Mrs. James. But why have you decided to sell?"

"I'm fighting too many people," she said aloud, thinking to herself, Yolanda, you see the truth. I'm fighting big Gulf Atlantic. I'm fighting the preacher. I'm fighting my neighbors. I'm fighting you. (It had come to her, Yolanda's serious face, broken up in laughter. But her granddaughter had not been laughing at her. She had been laughing with her, about the way the world is.) You want to be Yo. You gon' be all right, Yo, she thought. I see to that.

Upstairs, as he examined the steel engravings, the Tabriz continued to haunt Father Blouin. He returned to the parlor. Now that it was empty of everyone except the musicians, he noticed that all the furniture of this room was of that particular orange-toned cherry wood that appears even at 2 P.M. to be washed by a setting sun somewhere. The burled pieces, especially, imitated golden sun and shadow alternately in rippling rays across their rich fronts. A federal secretary, an upright tea table, a breakfront cabinet, and a fine breakfront bookcase each beamed back its own radiance.

And the carpet—a 12' 6" x 18' 8" piece—lay quiet and empty, awaiting the encounter. Parts of the magnificent rug were wearing thin. "Goodbye, Old South," he thought.

As he began to study it, a universe of golden geometry both abstract and concrete, both in nature and out of it, rewarded him. Thirteen banded borders of varying widths controlled and repeated exquisite forms, led the eye inward to the heart of the work, eight profoundly intricate inner divisions, themselves shook-out leaf-and-flower worlds of golds, greens, rusts, oranges, reds, and black.

"Enter each world separately," Father Blouin told himself. He could not take it all in at once. When he at last came to the center of the piece he found himself pinned to a small piercing black eye, a circle at dead center of the rug. The angular slant of the overall design and the light and shadow that played on the velvety wool brushed first one direction and then another, were hypnotic. Gaze at it long enough, and the eye at the center—an omphalos, a sinkhole, a black hole of infinity—seemed to be pulling all the rest of the rug into it at the speed of light. "No more banded borders, no more invincible worlds." He shivered. "It's all going, blurring, moving too fast toward that black hole." He stared at the hole.

The musicians closed the grand piano, packed their instruments and left, and he did not even notice.

Après le Déjeuner

"Brrr, it's cold," chirped all the tourists good-naturedly, clutching the bars of the seats in front of them. But their discomfort fled when the bus turned off the river road at a gigantic oak tree that was ablaze with tiny white Christmas lights.

"Welcome to Bonne Heure Plantation Fantasy!" called their guide in a loud voice.

"Ahhh!" they gasped. There were even strings of sparkle up and down the massive trunk and out on the great sprawling surface roots. It was sunset, the perfect time for a picture, and the camera buffs were let out of the bus to snap to their hearts' content. "What a beautiful picture! I definitely want a postcard of that. I want to use this on my Christmas cards."

Their guide, a young Service Leaguer, indulged them. This was an impressive spot, with the tree lights backdropped by the gigantic spread of lights at the plant. Finally she said, "All aboard now. There's more to see."

Father Blouin climbed on with the others. This season would be the last time anyone could see Old Harmony. All that history would soon be plowed under and in its place a network of pumps, pipes, smokestacks, cat crackers and engines hissing and roaring, would be processing chemicals from crude oil derivatives. Even now, bulldozers dozed in the shadows on the other side of chain link fences.

"Notice on the left," the guide pointed out, "what the plantation folks called The Dummy. It's the actual little locomotive that pulled the cane to the sugar house in open boxcars which you see hitched to it. It's sitting on its own single gauge track."

"Oh, how adorable!"

"All outlined in lights! How perfect!" More pictures were snapped.

"Bonne Heure has been shut down for fifteen years," the guide reminded them. "But the owners are careful to keep everything in pristine condition. And thanks to their cooperation and the creative imagination of Sissy Crocker, who is wife of Gulf Atlantic's Charles Crocker, this year we are able to provide this wonderful scene from the past decked out in Christmas splendor."

The great rectangular sugar house itself was outlined in lights from foundation to rooftop and all along the incline that once propelled mountains of cane into the factory's maw. The towering cranes that swung bundles of cane a ton at a time from the train, and later from giant cradles of cane trucks, were also outlined in lights. The distant water tower, the plantation bell, the lowly weighing station, all were ablaze. An electric monitor tolled the bell continuously.

"You're probably asking yourselves, 'How did all this come about?'" The Service Leaguer paused to flip a tape of Christmas carols that had been playing through the intercom. "Sissy was packing her miniature Dickens Village into a new storage area in their home, when she began to handle the pieces and examine them more closely. She has a marvellous collection which she has added to over the years to the extent of two hundred and fifty separate pieces." She made a little joke about the growing unmanageability of the collection, quoting either Sissy or her husband, that made everyone shriek. Father Blouin missed it. He had been looking outside the window. "Anyway, as she handled the little shops, houses, railroad station, tea room, factory, and whatnot, the idea suddenly dawned on her to recreate Bonne Heure and Old Harmony for one last time. She went to work, enlisting the aid of our Service League, and especially Solange Vaucoudrais, representing the city, to raise the money for this beautiful extravaganza, the Bonne Heure Plantation Fantasy. Gulf Atlantic also contributed a generous grant to our project. We hope to continue the project year after year, adding to it. Of course, Old Harmony is now owned by the company and it must be razed to make room for expansion. Next year, however, we plan to add a big bonfire on the levee that can be seen up and down the river."

They rolled on to Old Harmony. They slowly moved past the little frame church, as bright as if it had washed its robes and gone to glory. Its bell tolled electronically. Father Blouin's eyes were smarting. Greater Mt. Sinai had sold out, too.

"Isn't it just darling?" The bus agreed, nodding their heads and smiling. They passed the cemetery which, of course, was unlit. "So sad for Harmony," said the guide through this passage. The bus agreed, tears sprang up in many an eye. "But when you see the new beginning in Harmony Estates, and all the modern advantages the people have over there, you realize that everything has a happy ending. Everything turned out beautifully. Didn't it?" The bus agreed.

They were now turning up the lanes of row houses and new gasps of delight filled the bus. The weeds had been mowed by Gulf Atlantic. Every scraggly bush remaining in every dirt yard was lit. The burning bushes led the eye to houses, row on row, framed in light, including Niobe's, third from the end. Blouin lifted his eyes and met with a passing but transfiguring horror, a terrifying incongruence. The cabins looked to him like negatives of houses, all outlined in shining brittle white. The houses were X-ray'd black bodies and the roof ridges, windows, doors, porches and matchstick columns, looked like radioactive exoskeletons.

A freeze-frame from an Our Gang comedy struggled to get to the surface, and then to dominate, his mind. Buckwheat. Yes, the image was of Buckwheat electrified, his hair on end, scared white.

X and O

So I'm going Whaaa-t! I already missed my period by four days! And he goes like Naw, you're just...you're not. Are you? So go get checked out. Where? I dunno. The Public Health Department? And then, Are you knocked up, really? Well, I mean, its not that big a deal, is it? You messed up. No sweat. Only he's talking West Texas, Waaal, and real slow and all that, not like in California where I came from. Waaal, what did they tell you at the health department? Did you see one of themmm —counselors? I go Yeah. They get your name: O. Your age: 16. They don't tell you to do it or not do it. But they ask, like, "Can you support the baby?" Stuff like that.

And I tell him, it's all set up if I want it—. And then I go—I have to do something! I can't have it! I—we—can't have it! I'm saying this to X. And he goes Yeah, I know. And I go Yeah, you're right.

So we're all of a sudden in a panic to get it done. I want to do it today. I don't want another night of thinking about it, nightmares and all. Of course, they can't do it that quick. I sneak out of the house and telephone this clinic and make the appointment for Thursday, and feel better. Next day I cancel it without telling him. I can't. I can't. It's too terrible. It's a person, tiny as it is. It's on the way, coming at me in nightmares. But coming, for sure.

Jeeze, he was furious, you know, when he found out I canceled. He goes Why didn't we talk about it because by God he's involved too and it's his decision too. So I go You really don't care. I screamed about him having his fun and now look, and just get rid of it, huh—it doesn't mean nothing. Act like its a nothing! I'm a nothing! And like that. I mean, I sort of flipped out because I never have screamed at him and he had to close my mouth with his hand and throw me on the floor at his apartment. And I didn't care. Maybe that would make it come.

So then we got crazy and really tried to miscarry it. I went to a park by myself and jogged until I couldn't go any more. I hung upside down on the monkey bars, did push-ups and sit-ups. He knew a girl who had a vibrator—I don't know how he knew this girl had this thing. I was too shook up to think about it, and he wanted to go borrow it from her and try this—dumb, just like a guy. But I go No, what will she think? It wouldn't work anyway. Nothing worked. No way was it going to let go.

And I was still kind of wanting it anyway, it was kind of a nice feeling having it inside of me. It was ours.

But it was like three things kept crashing through all my thoughts. The three things hadn't ever been connected before and now they were like jammed into one. Sex, pregnancy, abortion. Sex gets you pregnant and then you either have it or do away with it. Sex-pregnancy-abortion. It was like beating into my head in my nightmares and all day in school. I... it didn't help in the girls' bathroom either—I mean, I would go in there, like to barf, but I never could, and would sit and strain hoping it would break loose, and there were three stalls and fuck on the walls of each one—no matter what one you went in—fuck-fuck-fuck. Three stalls, three fucks.

I would sit and remember him throwing French fries in the air and catching them in his mouth. I worked about two months in a place called French Fry City, it wasn't just fries but burgers and stuff and he got lots of practice waiting for me to get off. And the easy way he slid in behind the wheel all in one move. And we used to smooch at stop lights. Like tight together in the front seat of this supercab pickup he had. You could tell his pickup anywhere in town. He worked at a sparkle shop and he had done it all over in purple and gold metal flake, chrome mag wheels, chrome 10-inch drop bumper, headache rack, and running boards. It looked like a boat. What else? Yeah, a chrome rollbar and a light-bar with four lights, two amber, two white; and a shotgun rack. Not another one like it, and besides that, he had this bumper sticker "Ask me if I give a shit." That was him. That truck was him and he was that truck.

He was wanting to get a lift kit and convert it to a monster, but he went Yeah, he would use that money if we needed it to get it done, and borrow on his paycheck. And I had a little birthday money in the bank. It looked like he was beginning to not want us to get married. Not now, not ever. Ever. Ever and never. Forever and never. Those words ran around in my head, too. Words like Elsa Scott, our English teacher used. We used to get a really big yak out of her.

...Mr. Superslung. My girlfriend warned me he could kill you with his eyes. Watch you bleed. Like, he was drop-dead gorgeous. He still is. Really. But all that is gone. It was stupid anyway. It seems like it never happened.

So anyway... Oh. I guess I wasn't sleeping, I wasn't eating except nachos and Cokes. I would barely make it until I could get to a pay phone and call him. Then we wouldn't say anything. There would just be long silences and, Well, what are we going to do, and like that, and he would get jumpy and go Well I have to go now, back to work.

But anyway, we decided to go ahead and do it. Did I say that yet? That was the last thing we decided, anyway. Yeah, I go, you're right.

I just went "home" sick from school one morning and he drove me to the clinic.

It was a weird scene. It wasn't like any experience I ever had (my girlfriend, the one who warned me about X, said the same thing, she had one too); and God willing I will never have it again, but like she said we were up against it and there wasn't any other way out.

Tell my mom? She had me. My grandmother had her.

It was a normal looking place, like an office; shrubs and little trees, those kind of trees in office parks that never get any bigger. There were these Jesus freaks standing around in a bunch. Don't pay them no mind he goes when he helped me down out of the supercab and he took my arm, like rough, and gave them the finger.

Then, Oh God, he got a big goop of pink bubble gum from the parking lot stuck on the heel of his boot. We had to stop while he scraped it off with his pocket knife. It didn't want to come off. He had to scrape and scrape. God, Oh God. Here now, hell, don't pitch a fit in the street. It got all over his knife. He had to clean his knife on the curb. C'mon baby. You're gonna be glad after it's over.

He wasn't even there after it was over. At the beginning of it I had my sheet telling all about it; X paid the fee; I signed three forms; he had to go in the waiting room; it was soft colors, dusty rose and soft blue, and beige; it was kind of rich-looking, with magazines and all, but it was like fakey. They gave me blood and urine tests; a pelvic—flat on your back with your feet in these stirrup-things, he was asking like did I have any favorite rock stars—with his fingers feeling for something. Then we went to get counseled and she asked if we had any problems with our decision and nobody said anything; she did all the talking, telling all of what they were going to do, more than I wanted to know; taking care of yourself afterwards; using contraceptives. They must have a hard time not acting bored, there were so many lined up, exact same stuff over and over. That's all they did in there. Then you put on the gown and the paper shoes and then a counselor goes in with you and holds your hand if you want; all the while they were playing this soft rock, and now in the operating room or whatever they call it, when you go in you notice it suddenly has burst out louder to cover screaming or whatever; but I had made up my mind I wasn't going to freak out and I didn't. I just held the lady's hand tight and tried to shut out that frigging music.

He wasn't even there when I got through. It was the most alone I have ever been. He had a reason I found out later but I was really pissed and, you know, crying, when he wasn't there. He spun up in his brother's car like twenty minutes later. He started telling me all this stuff about moving the pickup. He was worrying about his pickup and that the Jesus freaks might damage it and all. How he moved it to the alley first, and then went back and drove it home and had to find his brother and borrow his brother's car, and I was hurting like hell and pissed off and then he said How'd it go? And I wanted to kill him or die myself.

No. I wanted it back. I go Give it back to me! I want it back! —It's funny, it's just like when I was nine my grandmother died, you know, the exact same thing, I screamed and yelled the same thing, I want her back! I want her back! They had to take me to her house, I made them take me to see for myself she wasn't there. And, same exact thing, I was empty inside and the whole earth seemed like a grave, and I burst out crying, and walked back and forth.

No, I was hobbling slow back and forth it hurt so bad and he stopped me from doing that and put me in his brother's car and took me to the apartment to rest until school was out and then I had to go home like nothing happened. Really. My brother was zapping zits in the bathroom when I got there and I couldn't get him out. Then I finally did and I changed the pad and went to bed for sixteen hours and I go, Just a bad period, to my mom. I got a big picture of telling my mom Gee, Mom, guess what?— My friend couldn't tell her mom, either. I mean, your *mom*. She had you.

I always had nightmares all through this, every night I got a nightmare. Then one night I dreamed it came back and it was real, I mean a real baby for sure and it smiled at me and...like—it wasn't a girl or a boy, it was just baby—I can't explain, it was like love showing itself to me. Like, it's okay, you know?

And he went That don't make any sense. It's in your mind. It was a goop of jelly. And I went Yeah, you're right.

I still get crazy, especially since we have split up. I still feel like a nothing. But I don't get any more nightmares.

Doucet's Last Paradox

The May cane was head-high, rippling green, twenty-eight thousand acres of it, held in the strong brown arms of the river. More intimately, at right angles to the river, Bayou Triste held only the town, crooked in its black elbow. The intervening lock between the waterways held back the river from flooding the small metropolis like an anthill. In spite of unspoken mutuality between man and nature that things would continue to hold, black underbellies of occasional clouds swept shadows across the land, deepening the green. Effluvia of chemical plants hung at the northern tip of the scene, edging closer. The death-dealing industries were moving in from the north. Salt water intruded from the south, destroying forty square miles of marsh each year.

But May labors went on. From the height of a hawk, the dirty river took on a silver-gray sheen. Wakes of tiny tugs and barges produced a watered silk effect. The spider web of the bridge spanned the banks of the bayou next to its companion, the train bridge. Busy black bugs moved to and fro in its meshes. From new building sites, the reassuring sound of hammers, and from backyards, family dogs' deep and confident barking.

And on this May Day Bosley Doucet lay between life and death in the local sanitarium. The doctor thought the stroke may have brought about Doucet's fall. He had fallen, taking out the garbage. The back of his head had struck one of the flat round stepping stones recessed into the earth of the backyard, and now he had a concussion. He was paralyzed on the right side of the body and had difficulty speaking. The doctor put it bluntly to Fiona that Bos faced a very real danger of "stroking out," and she accepted it impassively. Doucet had already asked forgiveness from his wife with his eyes but she had not granted it. She avoided his eyes. She had her pride.

His mind was clear and it noted yet another embellishment in the seemingly endless traipsing of tropes through his life: "He had laid the foundation for his own downfall." Melodramatic cant. "He himself had set in those flagstones." In this bit of irony the intensive/reflexive pronoun was employed correctly, and the reference was to himself in the third person. Years of teaching literature and empathizing with literary characters may have supplied these little stratagems, which distanced him from pain, his own and the pain he inflicted on his family. Now that his world had suddenly been reduced and projected onto a small convex screen, he felt more than ever that he was observing someone else's lifeline moving swiftly on the screen, represented by a miniature series of jagged green peaks and valleys.

As Doucet hung between life and death in Intensive Care, his household huddled near him, as though each was anxious to redeem a rightful piece of him: Fiona; his son Theo, called from college; his married daughter Lori. His mistress was expected momentarily, to say her goodbyes, plead her distant cloudy kinship, and claim her own meager portion. His wife, in a rare magnanimous gesture, had acknowledged that in a twenty-year-old affair some consideration must be given to the other woman. There had been precedents for this gesture in the French community. But no one had thought that *Fiona* would do it. Now the community knew that it was going to happen, even before

Althea left her front door. The church, the town, his wife, the greenest freshman in Bosley's class knew about Althea. It had been going on before that freshman was born, since Doucet was forty and Althea twenty-two. The people shrugged it off. It was French. It was the next thing to custom. The pillars of the town had mistresses. The only quirky thing was to think that little Bos, the quiet, the thoughtful fellow with the furrowed brow, laughlines around his eyes, the soft black beard that seemed to be threaded with spider webs—Bos had a mistress. And to think the mistress was that sweet little Althea Marks. The kids at school called them the Teenie-Weenies, with a certain affection, and often fell upon their surrogate bosoms for unburdenment.

For some time now, he and Althea had been content simply with each other's daily presence at school. They still met at her apartment very occasionally, never simply for sex, but sometimes sex happened. Now, closing his eyes, he felt her silken clean-shaven legs, lightly tanned, sliding over his own, against clean sheets. He heard the sound of their lips kissing in the dark. He would gladly have died like that, sighing in her arms, at that last meeting, or at any particular crux over the years, including the present moment, but the thought of death carried the counterthought of retribution.

Bosley's sixty-year-old mind rarely looked forward. Now, since he was probably going to die, his mind lodged in the past, specifically, on the picnic, the day they had discovered that they loved each other. He often referred his mind to the picnic on a day when everything else had gone to hell. It had been a May morning like this one. They had volunteered as English Department chaperons for the sophomore class picnic and were driving to the ruins of the antebellum place people called the Pink Castle. Althea was riding with him and three students in his VW bug. They followed the river road. A clover pasture flowed on their right, where rooted cows licked their newly thrown calves. Down in the clover the hundred-thousandth generation of working bumble bees thrummed like a mighty little string orchestra, promising to play on and on. Under the clover the earthworm nosed deep in the clean wet earth.

They paused at one point to explore a road that ran up the levee. From the top they viewed the broad river, the brown man playfully encircling the bulging waists of country towns with his muscled arms, then nonchalantly rolling off the face of the earth. In a pocket of the river, in a deep barrow pit, two groggy loggerheads had eluded for fifty years the wily Cajun's sharp hooks embedded on the underside of logs, designed to snag their soft parts. They now reaped their reward. Having reached sexual maturity at age fifty, this morning they discovered what makes the world go around.

Bos and Althea had explored the wreckage of the Pink Castle while the kids organized informal games at a nearby ballpark. There were no extraordinary words exchanged that day, no significant looks. But they were suddenly in love. There were no words to describe it. The rapture. The wholeness. The gratitude. Althea once said that whenever she thought of the picnic she envisioned God shaking the bright crumbs from His tablecloth over them. There had been precious few crumbs after that day.

He had not realized until that time how much self-mutilation had taken place in order for him to fit Fiona's marriage mold. She was once very attractive, darkly vibrant. He was once a whole person, in love with her. Now they lay nights under the heavy crucifix, bodies crossed randomly like two fallen columns of a ruined house.

She considered him a poor provider, unambitious, inept, uncommunicative, inattentive to her and the children. He thought that insecurity and pride ruled her emotions. A bad combination. Nothing could put her insecurity to rest. There was no secure place for her this side of God's bosom. And she would not be happy there, he thought wryly, in a place where there are no goods, nothing to buy.

Often they lay still except for the motions of their plotting minds, choosing the weapons for the next day. Once he lay thinking of similes of her unattractiveness: Fascinatingly ugly as a lava lamp. Inextricably ugly as scrambled egg trapped in Brillo—. "Humph!" she suddenly said. She seemed to monitor his very thoughts in her sleep. In his sleep he would groan, feeling dawn coming on. Often they didn't wait for dawn.

"You favor Lori."

"You say I favor Lori."

"You always favor Lori. You should do things with Theo—things he likes—football. He loves football."

"We play chess."

"That's not enough. He doesn't like chess as much as football."

"I'm not into football."

"You should get into it for his sake."

"Why are you bringing this up in the middle of the night? It's not even football season."

"It was so obvious last fall. I felt terrible for him. I'm telling you ahead of time, so you can be getting ready for it next fall."

"You always bring things up when I'm trying to get back to sleep."

"All the other fathers I know love it and they play touch with their kids, and go off together to games, and... You! Never!" *Always* and *never* frequently showed up in their conversations. "And I tell you, Bosley, Theo will never get to college if we don't plan better and put aside more."

"Fiona, we are scraping the bone." The outer Bos was a saver. His inner self was profligate as nature herself.

"We need to do more than we're doing. Mama..."

He drifted away, knowing she was preparing to quote her mother on thrift. Her mother in profile looked like Dante Alighieri, especially in winter when she wore a dark poncho and that flat velour sort of bonnet.

"...and if you said that to her, you're a damn liar."

He didn't know what he had said. He didn't argue. He had never been able to make himself understood. And, perhaps she was right about some things. Love had slipped away—she was always saying it was his fault; perhaps it was. Their marriage, once as lush and green as the canefields, was turning toxic. At best life was an endless loop, studded with monotonous knots of existence, daily battles against psychic pain. And what of their children at that time? Fourteen and ten years of age. One in flower, one in bud. The marriage wore at its points of strain: money, his failure as a provider, the children.

And then, Althea. The ravishment was something the lovers could do nothing about. They could have stopped the physical acts had one of them moved away from the other, but neither found the moral strength to do so. So it began.

After Althea, a gap had opened up between Theo and himself. One Sunday night they had set up for their chess game. Bos was moving out his first pawn when Theo calmly lifted the board and tipped all the pieces back into their box. "Game's over." He went to his room, picked up some essentials, and left the house. For the next year he lived with Fiona's mother. When he came back home, it was on his own unspoken terms. He and Bosley never touched.

After Althea, Bos and Fiona did not try anymore. "You could dump your whore in the river tomorrow," she told him. "It wouldn't change a damn thing." He knew it was true.

The hall of the sanitarium was crowded with visitors although it was only 8:30 on this May morning. Visiting hours were not honored except in Intensive Care. People came and went at will, drank black coffee, and smoked and talked in the halls. At times noise levels drowned out the intercom.

By silent assent the Doucet family was out of sight as she hurried past the people, whose mouths closed as if a dead hand had swiftly passed over them. She stepped quickly into ICU and across the threshold of his module, formed by removable wall panels with a curtain for a door. She drew the curtain behind her. She was a small, indistinct shape at first. The lines of resolution then sharpened about her and he saw her clearly: long straight blonde hair that was filling with gray now but which still reminded him of child-hair that had never known any care but washing and brushing. High sharp cheekbones, her face a disappointment—a complexion marred by acne pits—until she turned her face and her eyes flashed like bits of broken sky-blue cloisonné.

The back of his head was heavily bandaged. Attached to intake-output machines, various tubes and wires violated his nose, the vein of his left forearm, the skin of his breast, and under the lightweight spread, his urethra. They had taken him off the respirator. The tube in his throat had been pulled out, but he could not make himself understood. He made a sound in his throat, and she cried out loud in shock and grief.

Monsignor Blouin had been sent for, but Father Dudley Pitre came. Father Dud, who leaped out of bed every dawn with his fist upraised, exulting—"All for Jesus!" Fiona was disappointed. She had wanted more solemnity, more propriety. Monsignor would not get personal, and yet he could put the fear of God into someone. Father Dud—ha—Father Dud, he was a bull of a man, but he couldn't put the fear of God in a flea. They said he was the dumbest one in the seminary. He had to be the oldest one ever ordained from it. She showed him into Bosley's curtained cell and then vanished.

Blouin had once asked Dudley to correct him if he was wrong, but didn't Fiona Doucet wear the pants in that family. "Wear the pants?" Dud had snorted. "Hell, she wears the whole suit! Pants, coat, tie—jockey shorts! You're her spiritual advisor. Maybe she keeps it on a highfalutin plane with you, but I've heard confessions—" He had wanted to finish, "where all she does is throw shit at Bos," but the ban had silenced him.

Doucet rolled his eyes toward Dudley, struggled to speak, could not get the words out. "Al—Al—"

"—thea," finished the priest. "You want to make your Confession," he declared, squinting up and down through his thick trifocals.

No. He had really wanted to ask Father Dud if Althea might be called back. He couldn't make himself understood. Dud kissed his satin ribbon stole and threw it over his head, lopsided on his shoulders, a purple streak barely hanging on. He cast a wide and generous blessing at his penitent. His voice was very deep, Godlike. "The Lord be in your heart and on your lips, that you may rightly confess your sins. In the name of the Father, and of the Son, and of the Holy Spirit. Amen." Bos crossed himself with his left hand, then Dud took possession of it. "You may say the Confiteor silently."

He continued to hold Doucet's hand. After a few moments, he continued briskly. "Since your last Confession, which was...a number of years ago...?...you have committed a number of sins, hmmm, in relation to God, to your family, to your neighbor, to the Church, and to yourself, hmmm?"

Doucet nodded.

"We'll get you right with the Church first. That's easy nowadays." He chuckled. "We used to bear down hard on Sunday Mass and holy days, confessing once a year, servile work on Sunday, fast, abstinence, Holy Communion during Eastertime, contribute to the church, so on, so on. Today, blanket absolution. Blanket. I absolve you."

He walked Bos through the minefield of the Seven Deadly Sins and through the Commandments. Then they backed up for a closer study. "Now. In relation to God. Love of God above all things. Guilty?"

Doucet nodded.

"Doubts. Worldly fear. Murmuring. Lack of hope, or resignation. Resistance to grace."

Doucet saw on the page, "The priest had a keen, penetrating mind." Hell, no. He was a damn snoop. God's Private Eye.

"Neighbor, family. Love of neighbor for God's sake. Obstinacy. Hardheartedness. Lack of consideration, lack of charity. Hatred. Injurious words or actions. Forgiveness of injury. Lying. Incitement to sin. Injury to reputation. Debt...well, skip over debt. Yes? Debt? O.K. Forget irreverence. Yes? O.K. Skip calumny, backbiting, violence, theft, jealousy. —Backbiting? Backbiting, too? O.K." Bos was nodding yes to everything. The priest went on with a plodding tenacity, strip-searching Doucet's soul. "In relation to yourself. Practice of one's chief virtue. Eradication of one's chief defect. Let's look at pride. Dear God! Pride." Dud was getting worked up. "Now—there's a sin! Guilty? Sure."

Yes, nodded Bos.

Dud's face was red, but the anger was not directed at Bosley. "Everything stems from pride!" He slapped his gorilla chest once with his free hand and his voice powered up momentarily to organ register: "The sin from Hell. The mother of all sins. Jesus had to climb up on the goddam cross to pay for this one!"

Sinners in the hands of an angry Dud, Doucet thought. He smiled a little with the left side of his mouth.

Then silence. A swelling, gusty sigh from Dud. "—Sensuality in one's thoughts, looks, reading, conversation, actions. Bad example. Scandal." He paused for the briefest of moments. Doucet closed his eyes over hot tears. His lips formed the word yes. Then his mouth tightened again.

Aimer à la folie, thought the priest. Is it a sin, to love to distraction? No, only what follows. "How can we help loving?" he asked, suddenly gentle. "It's our nature to love. But we must remember our commitments.

"Now. Neglect of mortification. Anger. Skip self-sanctification. Vanity. Hmmm. You don't seem to have much ego, Bos. Skip greed, intemperance, gluttony, sloth. Impatience. Yes, impatience? Who isn't impatient? Intemperate, also, sometimes? Drink a little too much? Ah, dear God, yes we do.

"We will meditate for a few moments on any other sins which we have not confessed, or which you cannot at present remember." Doucet lay restless, mentally pawing through his box of troubles, spilling fragmented memories of the actions, words, thoughts of his entire adult life. One summer of his college years had been spent in Germany. He remembered vividly a scene from Grünewald's altarpiece at Colmar. Tortured souls entering eternal damnation. A trio of two men and a woman. The woman is going over the edge. The men try to drag her up from the brink by her hair. At the bottom corner of the panel a man is devouring his own hand. It is in his mouth to the wrist. The other hand twists his ear. This figure, this little Doppelgänger, had accompanied him through life, alongside the virtuous heroes of literature. Bos's right hand twitched, though it was paralyzed.

Nurses and aides kept popping their heads through the curtain and saying, "Oh, I'm sorry, Father." Dud tried to bring his basso down to a whisper, succeeded only in growling in Doucet's ear. "God loves you, man. He really does." He tightly squeezed Doucet's small hand into a little doughball, kneading it inside his big rough one. "For your penance, say the *Benedic Anima Mea*—Psalm 102. And now make a good act of contrition. May the Holy Spirit fill your soul with all the graces of the sacrament. God has His ear to your heart now. Talk to Him from your heart."

He could not make himself understood.

Father Dud rumbled the psalm for him, "...Bless the Lord, O my soul, and never forget all He hath done for thee," reading from a holy card fished from his inner coat pocket. He finished, "...For He knoweth our frame; He remembereth that we are dust."

He granted absolution. A nurse came in apologetically, took Doucet's life signs, replaced the i.v. antibiotic and body fluid pouches while Father Dud prayed. Dud then crossed himself over his broad vitals, blessed Bosley again, and gave him the viaticum from a little silver case.

In a few moments he roused himself from silent prayer and boomed cheerily, "Now I'll call in Fiona and the kids and we'll anoint you." A great laugh rose in Doucet's chest, but only a groan came out. They had always laughed and shrugged their French shoulders at Dud. "Oh, Father Dud. He's too oldchurch, he's a woolly mammoth." Sometimes they said, "He's too Vatican II, he's too fast, he's too raw." His manner was comic and...immaterial. Now he was in the role of dispatcher; no, expeditor. And yet Doucet was strangely comforted by his presence, like that of a brother.

They came in. Fiona was skinny and sleek and swarthy. Her mother's face flashed before him in cameo. Fiona herself had now taken on the dark harrier-hawk look and was become both wife and mother-in-law. Her deep purple lipstick played harshly against the sallow face drawn and set into a programmed configuration: bony nose more pinched than ever, scored lines around her mouth. Theo came in looking very solemn. Lori came with swollen, blue-shadowed eyes. She broke down again when she saw Father Dud, and cried on the priest's shoulder. What was happening seemed so unreal, she had not had time to take it in, to readjust her sunny life so quickly.

Fiona had brought the crucifix from the wall above their bed. She had also brought a candle and six pieces of cotton, one each for eyelids, ears, nostrils, lips, palms of the hands, and soles of the feet. She set these out on the bedside stand on a plastic cafeteria tray. Lori drew herself away from Father Dud, and onto her own father, crying.

"Lori, okay. Okay. I—love you—girl." It was the first time he was able to speak. She looked into her father's white face, neat-featured, soft-bearded, defenseless without the dark defining rims of its glasses. She had seldom seen it without its glasses. She sobbed again. He looked beyond her, to his son, staring until Theo finally looked at his eyes. He held out his left hand. Theo took it, and cried, holding his father's small hand to his cheek.

Father Dud swept up the cotton balls in one of his big paws and dropped them in the wastebasket. "The Church doesn't do the old rite of Extreme Unction anymore," he said. "We simply anoint Bosley's forehead with oil and pray for healing." He put the same big hand on Lori's shoulder and began. "Peace to this house." Answering himself, "And all who dwell therein."

Peace will come to the house when I am gone, thought Doucet. He had never experienced peace, but the thought that peace was now guaranteed to his family, the promise of it, yes, even to Althea, made him weak with happiness. The vibrant violet of Father Dud's satin ribbon beckoned like the strayed bar of a rainbow.

"Bosley." He felt something shaking his left foot. He had forgotten where he was, what he was doing on this bed. Fiona was sitting on the only chair in his cubicle, placed at the end of the bed. She was shaking his foot. "Bosley. I've been sitting here all day and I have to go home for a while with the children. Bosley, wake up. Can you hear me?"

He nodded and looked to the source of the voice. When she was sure she had his attention, she opened her battered black alligator purse. The zipper uttered a sustained excruciating whine end to end, as though she were ripping open an old wound along its scar. "Bosley. This is something we've never discussed. We have never picked out plots for ourselves." She bent over herself and rooted in the purse—it seemed to his heightened senses that she was ransacking her own uterus—for something she could not find. A great bubble of pity began to inflate inside himself. He pricked it with his mind. She pushed aside the small but heavy crucifix, the blessed candle she had brought for the last rites, and the cotton balls she had retrieved from the wastebasket, which were perfectly good and could be used again. She took out a brochure and a little hand-drawn map on a single sheet of paper.

"You know how expensive they are. Well, it so happens there are two spaces in Mama and Papa's plot. There is Papa's grave, and the place next to it for Mama. And two other spaces." She suppressed a sob that was threatening to explode. It imploded harmlessly inside her. "If it is all right with you, those will be our...our...places." He nodded. She started to point out to him their location on the map, but he shut his eyes. She thrust the papers back in her purse and suddenly crumpled and gave a shriek, a subdued shriek because she did not want to be put out of Intensive Care. "What are we going to do if...if...? —How are we going to live?" She wrenched her head up and stared into his eyes for the first time since he had been hospitalized. He knew that financial panic was the catalyst for her shrieking. He tried to give her a look that, while it could not possibly convey love, was consoling, replete with fiduciary assurance. He must have managed such a look, for she composed herself again. "I am praying for you, Bosley. And I will always pray for you."

His face immediately darkened with fear. Please God, No. He must escape her finally. Even if it meant sending his soul—God knows where—he mustn't be in her prayers. He struggled not to appear to cast her out, not to commit the final sin, was it of pride? Yes, the mother of sin. But the words flew up into his mouth out of fright and hubris. His lips tried to form them. "I don't want to be in your prayers."

He could not make himself understood. He tried and tried to say it aloud. It would have given him sovereign satisfaction to say it. He imagined himself saying it, and her reaction. She would be cut to the quick. The ultimate rejection. She would scream, "Damn you, then!" She would point out how she allowed his whore in here to see him out of the goodness of her heart. She would furiously rescind a thousand things she had done for him, enumerate all her sacrifices and humiliations, all the things she had suffered through and done without. The room would have been filled with the black bat-winged demons of her recriminations. Most of all she would denounce her offer to pray for him. His self-imposed sentence would have capped all her bitterness—that one sentence.

He struggled again to say it. "I...I—." He was not to be allowed to say it.

"I know, Bosley," she said, satisfied, as if she were again, after all the years, in full possession of him, her hand lightly on his feet, shackling his feet in their twitchings. She watched the workings of his face.

In spite of himself, his body gradually relaxed. Suddenly, a pervasive warmth inside like warm wings fanning ashes to life. He felt all his resistance melting away in the warmth. The world as he knew it was passing away. He seemed about to be vested with a new personhood. It was impossible not to respond. He abandoned himself. O God, be merciful to me, a sinner.

The day of the wake was absolutely gorgeous. Some springs, Louisiana outdoes even herself with magnolia, bougainvillea in furious bloom, and passion flower (called by the children "Maypop"). Above the funeral home a mockingbird swung at the top of a fuzzy green sapling like an acrobat on a sway-pole. Buzzards drifted on thermals, at work when they seemed not to be. Purple martins darted, their wings cut the air like scissors, clipping off the lives of early-morning mosquitoes. Backyard sounds, the distant barking of dogs, alternated with persistent tapping, the overlapping metronomes of carpenters' hammers.

The two most pressing needs, a burial plot and the funeral service, had been taken care of. Monsignor Blouin was to say the High Mass. Her husband's mistress would not view the body. She might attend the funeral, as a colleague, or she might not, at her discretion. The two women's struggle for dominance had become ritualized like those mating patterns in nature in which rivals avoid actual physical contact. They continued to honor the ritual even though the reason for it had been removed.

Fiona sat with her face arranged. She desperately clutched her purse as she would a lifeline. Mr. Niveleur, the undertaker, had relieved much of her care by his neighborly but efficient handling of arrangements, and now he gravely met guests at the door with a fistful of black pens, invited them to sign the register and keep the imprinted ballpoint with the compliments of the flourishing establishment. Working hardest when he seemed not to be, he periodically smoothed his metallic-gray hair, adjusted his cravat, impeccably tied and then pooched out just a little in the best embalmers' manner, and then ushered people into the proper parlor. One of Fiona's friends brought her a soft drink from the refreshment bar. A steady stream of friends, a surprisingly large number, perhaps a majority of the white people in town, and all of his students, black and white, filed by to pay their respects.

"How do you think he looks?" was the most popular question, as it is at most wakes. "He looks like himself." This was the answer that many gave. Some said, "He looks peaceful." The next most popular question, "How do you think Fiona looks?" brought forth these surprised replies from almost everyone: "Not bad!" "*Bien!* She's taking it hard but she's holding up well." "She almost looks pretty." They paused to speak to Bosley's family and to mourn the misfortune of the second clot which had made its way to the brain and taken his life.

Fiona distractedly shifted and resettled her purse, in which she had secreted half a dozen of the funeral home pens. She held her purse tightly on her lap in the same chair all day until nearly 3 P.M. Then, according to custom, she was to take a sleeping pill, repair to her bedroom, and try to forget her grief in sleep. She took two sleeping pills with another Coke and found the pills beginning to work on her before she left the funeral home. Noting her shakiness, Mr. Niveleur hastened to see her to the door. He held her arm. The other hand, autonomous, in an almost imperceptible gesture of mortmain, claimed her kidney. She felt woozy and detached, even slightly venal. And so, by some sleight of countenance, she quickly scribbled a wan smile between the lines of her face when the mortician's hand tightened around her rib cage, persisted there, at the front door, for just a moment too long.

See to Appreciate

"Hit that roach—there! Big one! Hit him. Get him. Crackerjack!"

"Got him. Lord, I think I've killed Kafka. Poor Kafka."

Kenny grins, sitting in the living room of a rent house belonging to his grandparents, Preston and Idylla Puckerbush Pratt. He has the same grisly grin as his grandmother, wider than it needs to be. He is sitting skinny and exhausted, forty years old, on a folding chair, like laundry lapped flat over the backrest and seat, in a very loose interpretation of his grandfather.

He's grinning at Jack. "What are you doing with that hammer, anyway? Going to knock off a piece?"

"Hush! I'm hanging curtains. Then—I might knock off a piece." Jack is small and dark, sports a B-movie moustache. "Oh, damn it all. I need to go to the crummy store for more rods. Don't have enough to finish."

"O.K., Crackerjack."

"What do you need? Anything?"

"Nope."

"O.K. Off to the crummy store." He kisses Kenny briefly and straightens the couch cover, noting that it needs washing again.

But he would wait for the next accident. Kenny follows him out the door like a puppy, meets the mail carrier, and collects the mail. He calls up the street to Jack. "You got a letter from Vancouver! From Jackie!" Jack pumps his fist.

Kenny returns inside, hits the TV remote, and takes a well-worn pack of cards from his shirt pocket. He lays out a game of solitaire on the coffee table as he sits on the couch and watches a newscast showing Bosnian mothers. They gesture, beseech the camera's face, pressing handkerchiefs to their mouths, holding back the wailing. Kenny cries. Tears spatter the cards. He isn't crying for himself. He is crying for the world, for women in shawls watching their men march off to become a curious detail in a carpet of bodies. He's crying for Jack. Jack has AIDS, too. They assume, for sanity's sake, that each had contracted it independently before they met.

He brings out the cards and watches TV only when Jack's not around. It drives Jack up the wall to see him so inactive. What a change from the way he ran around at the Peaceable Kingdom. The land, near Los Alamos, wasn't officially his—a patron had let him use part of his farm. It was just an encampment of tents at the beginning, another protest movement against nuclear arms, but it had had several good years, shutting down after the Cold War ended.

Jack had a very different background. After getting married and beginning a solid career in investment banking, he had suddenly divorced his wife of twelve years and turned over everything to her out of exquisite guilt for having played on her and the children the joke nature had played on him. It is something he lives with. Since he met Kenny one summer at the camp, he is able, most days, to see his sexual identity as a great blessing, not a joke.

As Jack steps out of the salvage store—the crummy store—his eyes seem to be playing tricks on him. Is that the Pratts' car crawling up the street? Of course, those two skeletonized figures inside, at ninety and eighty-four years old respectively, couldn't be any other two bodies on earth. It must have once been a point of vanity to Preston that he is six years younger than Idylla. Now it is a bad joke.

They had come to the house only once, to let him and Kenny in, but he would never forget them. Looking at them was like looking into hell.

They were born to be honored, to lend status, to dig ground with spades, to grandstand, to receive. They were always in the newspaper, standing in reception lines extending their dry philanthropic fingers, but only to the deserving, such as: the alumni fund at the local college where Dr. Pratt was Dean for so many years; the DAR; the Eastern Star, of which Mrs. Pratt is Worthy Matron; the First Christ Church building fund, of which she is a Stewardess; her college sorority, of which she was a foundress; and the Moral Majority—all of which will enjoy equal shares of the Pratts' total net worth.

Jack used to paint, and, recurringly, he wants to paint the Pratts. At this moment he poses them at a United Daughters of the Confederacy affair acknowledging Mrs. Pratt's many contributions to the lifeblood of that organization. There—the United Daughters have set her down in a gilt chair, as she can't stand up any longer. At her right is Dr. Pratt. His voice as he acknowledges the introductions is high and thin. With the inevitable shortening of the vocal cords, he and Mrs. Pratt exchanged voices as they aged. His voice weaves lightly about her gravelly bass-baritone that shades to basso.

Flatulent Dr. Pratt, flat as a mat, dainty as a cat, a head upon a stick, a hollow reed bent rigidly forward. Under a yellow moustache his own large preternatural teeth in self-mockery pass themselves off as a smile—Jack would daub gobs of yellow and white here. Pratt seems to have been handsome once in a generic way, but the colors of his personality, never bold, have bled into each other. No color is distinguishable now, he is a Gobelin tapestry gone bad, ruined by lifetime exposure to the worst of the elements.

Now her. She looks as old as the Confederacy. Her hands have a mind of their own. They move forward all the time, as if urging her on—Go! Go!—against the drag of her body. At ninety, she is an unwrapped mummy, everything shrivelled away except her teeth, receded and reclothed in a pair of great cloudlike sleeves to which is attached a dress. Jack sees the dress as rich moiré and brocade the color of old crochet, or new crochet that has been soaked in tea to age it. A couturier winding sheet twisted around her frame, it ends up in a giant bow at the back. Her hair, black as the bottle from which it comes, is also pulled back to a huge taffeta bow at the nape of her neck. In front, he sees a reptilian dewlap, a crepy curtain of flesh, swinging from her chin. She is at once strange and chic, ghastly and terribly terribly familiar to the other old Daughters attending her. She doesn't, can't, hear what they are saying. "She's right pitiful now," they say to one another. She grins.

Now he sees them coming closer, painted into their Sedan de Ville, seemingly on a Sunday drive, but in reality headed for eternity. Some way back, they'd let God know that they were satisfied with Him and would let Him know if things changed. The Cadillac now is lifting off the highway and is ready to sail into the skies. Lift-off point is where he would capture them on canvas. The caption: "Come unto my father's house?"

The car is cautiously feeling its way toward him. He suddenly leaps toward it, waving his arms and shouting "Hey! Hey! Hey!" in their faces. The windows are up, their deaf ears can't hear him anyway, they almost surely don't recognize him. Or maybe they do, and after the first flash of recognition they do not dare look again. If they looked something would have to be done. Startled and adrenalized, Preston speeds away and around the corner. "Shit!" says Jack three times, stressing the voiceless *sh* and *t*, spitting the word after them like an impulse sprinkler.

When he gets home, the letter from Jackie calms him. He reads it to Kenny and smiles. "God, I love that kid. He's just like his mother."

There had been no curtain rods of any kind at the salvage store. But he had bought up a complete closeout on wall paint and brushes. He tells Kenny about his encounter with the Pratts as he nails the rodless canvas curtains directly to the window frames. "I wanted to bang on their windows. If I'd had this hammer in my hand..." He climbs down from the chair he is standing on and grabs another panel of canvas. "I don't know why I keep trying to make an impression on those two old farts. It's the way they turned their back on you, after they raised you. You should have been their one treasure of life, and they threw you away."

"They rejected my mother, too. That was how I knew instinctively it was them and not me in the wrong. And as long as I did their shit it was fine. When I did my own thing, they turned me out."

"I wish they could see us like we are."

"Jack, they weren't overjoyed to see me the first time, when they had to take me in. Even less, the second time, when I came back from New Mexico. With AIDS. I mean, what's the point?"

"Family healing is the point. I know what it meant to see my kids last time in Vancouver. We said goodbye. It was sweet and wonderful. It was worth all the pain. Kenny, sometimes I at least want to collect the perfect moments we've had, and, like, write the Pratts a letter, or make a manifesto of it, our right to love!"

"Yeh."

"And hammer it to that big oak door of theirs." He buried a brad in the windowframe with one stroke.

"Yeh, like Martin Luther. The 95 Theses of Our Love."

Jack gave him a love look and a thumbs-up.

"Seems like I remember something about the Pope having to call the Diet of Worms...."

Jack collapsed in laughter. "So let the Pratts eat worms, too, I say."

Kenny fingered the pack of cards in his shirt pocket. "It's not that they're stupid. And it's not a religious attitude—they basically don't give a damn about God. It's pride. It affects their standing in the community."

"It was a shock to their whole system, sure, but most people accept it sooner or later. The Pratts never did." Jack's tongue was honed. "A Dean simply couldn't stand for it, you know. And how did he get to be Dean? He just trotted around the campus sniffing the right trees—where all the other Deans lifted their legs." He wanted to say a lot more, but didn't. "Well, one thing— it's made me want to paint again. I'm going to start right in when I get done with these curtains. I want to cover every square inch of this dump. Look! I got a free painter's cap with the brushes I bought."

"Go for it."

He paints all that summer. Few people come to the house, a crumbling 1930's stucco that looks as if an archetypal mammy had poured her great cauldron of grits over it and left it to age and yellow to the color of puppy vomit. Jack paints in his briefs with his painter's cap backwards on his head. Kenny sits within the sweep of the fan, plays solitaire. Acknowledging to himself that Kenny is too weak to do anything else, Jack suffers it. Once he walks in on Kenny watching snow after midnight. He clicks the remote and the image swallows itself. Now they don't watch much TV. Instead, Jack plays a lot of music, from Beethoven to Charlie Mingus plucking the guts out of a bass, to jungle drums, while he paints. They need to talk, they can talk above the music and through the painting.

"One summer, when I was twelve, I guess, I spent the summer with the Pratts. Idylla came up to my room above the garage and found the kid next door and me naked and diddling around. She sent him home and hauled out the Bible. She forced me to my knees and made me swear on it that I would never, never sin that way again."

"Not the first time the Bible has been used to abuse a kid."

"I was hoping she wouldn't tell Preston about it, but what the hell, she tells him everything. He whipped me. Bad. It was like he was punishing me just for being there, for being born, and my mother for having me. He never let that kid come around again. He wasn't quite the same to me even that summer. After I came to live with them, and he satisfied himself that I was gay, he never again treated me like anybody kin to him."

"Shiiit," says Jack. He thinks but doesn't say, They make my parents look like saints. He says, "My heartbreak, you know, was with Cindy. God, she loved me, unconditionally. She would not have left me even though she knew I was gay. I left her."

Kenny says, "Here's a woman who could have been truly bitter and vindictive. And she didn't even try to take you to the cleaners. You just gave it up to her and the kids."

Jack looks smaller and darker. "She didn't want the money. All she ever wanted was a loving husband."

When they talk the painting goes better. He paints as long as his strength lasts during the day. When he feels particularly strong, he paints at night with all the lights blazing. He starts with their furniture, salvage and thrift store rejects that had found their final reincarnation. He paints all the wood or pressed wood pieces, the plastic and chrome pieces, even the formica tops, in bold colors and folk motifs. On the kitchen cabinets, plump white and barred rock chickens roosting in jolly green dancing trees. Along the molding of the ceiling, verdant serpentine vine-and-leaf designs, half-concealing heavy bunches of grapes. Corn plant and wheat grow up the legs of tables and chairs. He paints Rousseau-like jungle scenes on the canvas curtains. After the furnishings he paints the living room floor with marine paint. Red. The smell makes them very ill. When they feel better he starts right in on the walls. After that he will do the ceilings. Kenny watches him. Glancing back at him one morning, Jack remembers how rounded and rosy he used to be. Cherubic.

"Listen to Mama. Eat it all. There's a picture in the bottom of your bowl." Hunched over breakfast, what he calls his mulch and milk, Kenny is birdlike, seraphic, but Jack is grateful for little things, that he himself can work, that Kenny can eat cereal again.

There is no real appetite for anything except painting for Jack and solitaire for Kenny.

Late at night Jack sits on Kenny's futon working long slivers of bamboo. "It's an immobile now. It'll turn into a mobile. Wait'll you see it." They turn out the light and hold on to one another. They marvel how each has grown so thin. Jack gently runs his hands over Kenny's limbs and torso, gives him his nightly massage. He kisses the sore joints tenderly. "Baby."

Kenny answers the gesture: "These bones say, 'I love you.'"

They habitually run a month late with the rent. Soon they are two months in arrears because Jack buys oil-based enamels, acrylics, and more brushes with the July rent. With the August rent, paid the first of October, Jack breaks down and sends a terse note. "If you would like to visit, mid-mornings and early evenings are best." He is thinking of their fragile state of health. Even though he has stated to Kenny many times that Idylla Puckerbush Pratt will outlive the vultures, he knows that they are all looking down the same road, and he adds, "I imagine that might be best for you, too." He receives in return a receipt for the rent.

The Pratts would prefer that they didn't communicate. Frail as they are, small upsets like Jack's note spoil the day. The rent they are collecting from the property is just a fraction of what it should bring. They don't like it that Kenneth and Jack are delinquent over token rent, but it can't be helped. It reinforces the mind set that Kenneth and Jack are just like the other deadbeats who populate many of their rent houses, their payments always late or nonexistent.

Idylla longs for their financial minds to be at ease. Impossible while these rent houses haunt them. Someone will have to be hired to take over. Or else the houses will have to be sold, starting with the one Kenneth and Jack live in. Selling this particular property nags her waking hours, especially every bedtime, like tonight's, that could be their last, when they might be drawing the heavy drapes for the last time in the fine old parlor with its Regency tables, bombé chest, Sheraton chairs and thick Aubusson rug. Even the cards nag her. Her hand shakes and jerks forward to place a red ten of diamonds over a black jack—the profile with its cavalier moustache is like Jack's.

Preston reads her thoughts and yells them back at her. "We'll sell the house after..." he trumpets and jerks his hands up and down irritably. "We won't want to be reminded..."

"Would anybody buy it, after...?" she shouts hoarsely.

"Who's to know?"

"Hah?"

"Who's to know? That level of people don't know anything." They pant in concert.

After this burst of unaccustomed emotion, she turns back to the game. She makes it, she had never believed you could make it when the last card turned up is an ace, but there it is, she has always been lucky at cards. Her blood pressure is up from the anxiety over the property. Her head is buzzing and ringing.

A faraway alarm clock goes off in her head and she thinks it is ringing upstairs in the room over the garage. The boy slept with his clothes on: baggy long shorts and a sack of a shirt. When the alarm went off he must have shoved his bare feet into loafers and tied a rag around his head so he wouldn't have to comb his hair, and he was ready for class at the small college where Dr. Pratt had been Dean. In winter his garb was a pair of jeans and a yellow hooded sweatshirt that obscured his face. Over that a ragged striped serape. He had come to them unbidden in his mid-teens. They had had another boy in mind when they took him in, an entirely different boy, whom he resembled less and less until he turned out completely wrong. The world went wrong then, and even God was suspect. It was a terrible scene when Kenny told them. Dr. Pratt was so angry, he seemed on the edge of a stroke. He kicked Kenny out "for everyone's sake." At the end she had wavered, to Kenny, "Are you saying...are you saying God made people this way?" Kenny had just smiled downward and said, "I'm saying God made people every which way."

He went off to New Mexico and they were sorry when he came back, bringing only trouble, like his mother did with her alcoholism and promiscuity.

The buzzing again. "Did you hear an alarm clock?" Idylla asks. "Your ears are ringing."

When the next month's rent arrives, there is only the $75 and no note. She is relieved, even to the point of shouting her relief to Dr. Pratt, and he shouts, thinly but firmly, that he, too, is relieved.

Nevertheless, when Dr. Pratt is asleep, she picks up the phone and calls the house, for the first time. To her shout: "Jack! How is he?" he tries to reply in detail, but she is too deaf or agitated to understand. Finally Jack shouts, "He's too weak to wipe himself. That's how he is."

"Is there somebody to see about him?"

"Me. I see about him."

"Idylla?" Kenny asks.

"Idylla. She couldn't get off the phone fast enough."

"At least she called."

"Manners. In the South manners take the place of heart."

"Manners are better than nothing." He turns his head away slightly and shrugs. Jack wants to touch him but something says no to that and to his next urge, to beat the wall. He goes back to painting. He puts on Beethoven's Fifth, stabs the wall with paint. No muted tones now. The colors scream, the four-note theme hammers. "Knocking on the door, man," Jack mutters. "We are knocking on the door."

The October rent money is paid in November to Pest Control Consultants, to exterminate the roaches, which will return in January. The pesticide makes them very ill. Christmas comes and they share it gratefully with a few friends and people from the hospice. The roaches return.

February. An unexpected thing happens. Jack dies, of pneumonia. A bad cold had hung on, gotten steadily worse after Christmas, until his breathing became labored and his feet and ankles so swollen, Kenny called for help. Someone from the hospice took Jack to the emergency room. His heart failed and he died before they ever got him stabilized and into Intensive Care.

A hospice volunteer now cares for Kenny mornings. What she thinks of the painted interior she keeps to herself. None of my concern, her face says to Kenny. Maybe she was forewarned. Landlocked on the futon, he exults in past moments of time that metamorphose into living beings on the walls. These glowing revisions of earth and cosmos had been their joint property, now Jack had deeded them over to him.

He turns his eyes on the hospice lady to rest his mind from the memories. Too bad Jack couldn't paint her as a tourist in his paradise. Her pants are bulging polyester in faux herringbone. She's a study in polyester patterns, cheap turtleneck knit pullovers with gaudy flowered blouses on top. She grunts to get down to his level on the futon. Spooning soup into him, or tucking in a corner of the blanket, she might have been merely death's advance agent, she needn't have caught his eye while carrying on her kindly patter. *Caritas*, he thinks.

His own death takes place in her presence, for which they both are very grateful, his wasted head on her bosom of flowers.

When the Pratts recover from their mourning or whatever that period of adjustment might be called—someone said they could not suffer because they didn't know how—they inspect the property. They had heard things about it.

From the shady, shabby old street the property presents to their view: a new blue housefront like a backdrop representing an indigo pre-morning sky, blued cloud shafts fringed with gold and red streaking toward a giant rising sun circling the door, a giant ruddy ascending sun drawing them in at tremendous speeds, to its fiery heart. They enter the house through the molten core, not even seeing the brilliant totem figures painted on the porch columns that warn through their grinning teeth, We are your ancestors. Enter at your own risk.

The red floor of the living room dazzles their sight at first.

Then they stare at a great geometric wheel laid down in red, gold, and black paint that dominates the scarlet ground with cycles of marching zigzags, lozenges, hooked diamonds, stylized animals, serrated leaves, palmettes, medallions, and rosettes. It resembles a Hopi sand painting. It resembles an Aztec calendar. It resembles a Qashqa'i tribal carpet years in the making. The bands race around and around, dizzying Idylla so, she must find a chair. She slumps back in the chair, looks straight up, and points wordlessly to the ceiling. On the ceiling is a full-length figure of a sleeping man with a swarthy face, but the face is, strangely, Kenny's. He is lying under a throbbing white moon with faint glyphs on its surface. He is in a desert place, barefoot, clad in a striped serape. He is sleeping so hard the eyelids are slightly raised and the pupils slightly to one side. Lying with him is a beautiful guitar, and beyond that, at guard, a lion couchant.

The Pratts rally and get up from the chairs. The kitchen presents only minimal shocks: brilliant yellow walls, cavorting chickens in folk scenes, green grapevines, lascivious-looking clusters of purple grapes, an old commercial Maytag washer in flesh tones with painted hands clasped comfortably under its glass womb. But when Idylla swings open the pantry door, she jerks back and screams. Roaches! Two cockroaches rampant, perfectly rendered, shiny black, four feet tall, are poised to spring at her from the back of the door. The Pratts react with horror and fear, but also with growing anger. They are beginning to realize that their property has been trashed. They don't want to look, but they are drawn hypnotically room to room to see things that have been hidden from them from the beginning. It is as if they fell down a hole and came out in wonderland. Or hell.

Over the door of the bedroom is inscribed: "Man is least himself when he talks in his own person. Give him a mask and he will tell the truth."—Oscar Wilde. The bedroom as they enter is dark. The walls and ceiling appear to be black. Preston turns on the wall switch. Black lights illuminate a chamber of horrors as their aged vision turns onto the most terrifying faces they have ever seen, the stuff of nightmares painted right on the walls. The bedroom furniture has been pulled away from the walls to a central island on which Kenny's slatted futon perches like a beached outrigger. Directly over his bed hangs a great open split-cane mobile that turns slowly in the mauve light, and out of that purple glow painted masks jump at them, so many they overlap one another: dripping heads taken in trophy, faces that are barely recognizable as human—hybrid creatures, part man, part animal, strange beaked creatures, muzzled forward-thrusting faces with monkey ears. Packed in with these are three-dimensional masks of styrofoam and papier maché, flatplaned faces gazing upward, countenances aggressive and bulbous, round, conical, rectangular, or elongated. Some faces are reduced to austere geometric equivalents, two holes here, a slash there. They are silent. They scream.

Idylla is alternately muttering "Oh, no! Oh, no!" and pressing the heels of her hands to her mouth. Then she shouts at him. "AIDS! It's the Mark of the Beast! They had to be Satanists!"

"No, no, Idylla!" he shouts back. "I've told you all along, they were on drugs. These are obviously hallucinogenic paintings. Dopeheads! They were dopeheads."

"And Satanists!"

"Posh!" Dr. Pratt's belief in the dominion of God, paltry as it was, was infinitely stronger than his belief in the dominion of Satan. But he didn't argue with her.

The whites of eyes seize the light and bewitch the Pratts' own eyes in their faltering tour of the room. Right to left, left to right, straight ahead, round or slanted, the eyes of the masks follow them, wild, on stalks, in aggressive beetle-browed accusation, confrontation, stark terror. Under sprouting topknots of raffia the eyes are evil slits, the whitened faces end savagely with open mouths and bared teeth ready to eat Dr. and Mrs. Pratt. There are funerary masks worn to dance a great one safely to another world. Other dance masks hang here: heads for harvest ceremonies, heads on sticks used for grave markers, to delineate the dancing ground, for door entrances, or as royal maces in sacred shrines taboo to all but adult males. Beyond these, ferocious Tiki war gods, masks for circumcision, for male initiation rites, for exorcizing demons, for the installation of a king.

At the other end of the spectrum, some are deeply carved, half-lidded in suffering; some are studies of liquid black pupils in abstract gazes of meditation, peace. In every face is some element of Kenny's physiognomy, fantastically rendered. His own look is there, sometimes laughing or smiling as in the old days like a jolly Buddha. Sometimes his long thin neck is coiled round and round in rings, the flesh of his face is scarified in whorls over his broad forehead, in labyrinthine scrollwork over his full cheeks. Down the bridge of his aristocratic Puckerbush nose, a keloid ridge. His teeth are filed to points.

Idylla staggers around in baby steps and Preston quickly turns away. He modulates his voice so she can't hear him: "Disgusting low-life bastards! They have ruined this house."

He goes about what he has come to do. Calculations. Front b.r. 201.5. Same for back b.r. L.r. 270. 2-2-1. Hardwood floors throughout. Stress this. Spacious. Handyman's Delight. Established neighborhood. Close to busline. No, near busline. Saves a word. Convenient to hospital, shopping center (make that mall), schools. Excellent rental possibilities. Price negotiable. So...let's see...Completely renovated. No. Updated. Or, newly repainted. Neat and clean. Cute, cozy stucco. No. Old-fashioned comfort. See to appreciate. Large trees on property. Separate, one-car garage. No, unattached. Or leave garage out completely. Yes, best to leave it out.

The last face, the one all the faces seem evolved into, is painted to simulate ivory of great age. It is a beautifully serene countenance of closed deep-set eyes, a death mask from which the mask has at last been removed.

The fourth wall is black.

They turn to escape from this bizarre sanctum sanctorum. They look back to Kenny's bed and then up to the great serene mobile, as if for deliverance. It is a triangle, a blowup of the Polynesian navigator's stick chart by which he set his course. The open, three-dimensional cane strips are crossed by other bleached cane parabolas, intersecting sets of parallel lines, and precisely placed angles, studded at certain points by small white shells. Once, it faithfully reproduced the swells and currents under his boat and around the islands represented by the white shells, steering him to the unseen land.

Over the futon in the black night certain fixed stars shine through the latticework of the stick chart. In the distance can be seen other landmarks: pillars of cloud, which always rise above the peaks of volcanic islands, and dots that might be seabirds on the endless windlass of their flyway, and far to the east, gray sky lightly washed to faint aquamarine, the reflection of a shallow lagoon lapping onto a jewel of an atoll.

The Pratt feet are locked to the floor as they gaze up to the mobile. They do not blink for a moment. "It's a Satanic symbol," whispers Idylla half to herself, forgetting to shout it for Dr. Pratt's hearing. But he knows what she is saying.

"Idylla, don't worry. None of this can touch us or hurt us. It will all be cleared out and cleaned up, I promise you." He grasps her arm in the vise of his own. "Come on, we're leaving now. Come on."

She cannot stop staring at the mobile, its maze of crossings, its turning almost imperceptible in the still air. Her hands are beseeching Go! Go! She looks up and up at it and squints over miles and years. What am I trying to see? I don't know. "What is it? What is it?" she begs, her voice cracking sharply.

Preston is guiding her back through the living room. Working fireplace. No. Fireplace. Spacious living room. Hardwood floors. She is walking slowly backward, staring up at Kenny sleeping in the striped serape, strange, surreal, and peaceful, and she staggers a little as she walks backwards in Preston's grip, looking up. He turns her around gently but firmly.

They are at the front door, nearly escaped, when they

confront themselves on either side of the door. There she is, replicated as a blackskinned Solomon Islander. A long slender bone pierces the nasal septum but the Puckerbush nose is unmistakable, as is her grin. Wild and beautiful, she is fabulously tatooed in many colors from crown of head to dewlap to the slatted rack of her chest with its breasts limp as Dali's watches. She is holding a fiercely protective arm around a tiny baby—a little black cherub—on her hip.

But him. Unmasked, his severed head flows down into a reptilian creature serpentine about the entire doorframe, whose scales end at fingers which are pulling down his own mouth cavity in a scream.

Idylla resists, but Preston forces her through the front door. Halfway through the passageway, she shrieks and collapses backward into the living room.

The shock was too much for her, they said. She died of outrage. She died of shame. She died because it was her time. She died from richness. She was scared to death. She died of envy. Well, said the hospice woman, it's plain what happened. She had to go back through herself to get out of there.

There are many theories on it, nothing definitive.

One of the last acts of Dr. Pratt's life is to have the furniture hauled away and junked, the floors stripped, the house painted over inside and out, requiring many coats, and the property put up for sale according to the last wishes of his wife.

See Ya Later, Floydada

W hat other state could have such towns: Clyde. Claude.
Clint. Clute. That place you like to see in your rearview
mirror. The one with the roadside population sign showing 1121,
topped by a sparrow being topped out by another sparrow,
signifying all there was to do in that town which, if it wasn't
named one of the above, might have been called Flatonia, New
Deal, View, No Trees, Cut and Shoot, Sour Lake, Earth (Arth),
or Muleshoe.

Or Floydada, located north of Quanah Parker's great canyon,
where he rode in black paint with his war bonnet trailing the
earth; Floydada perched on its shrivelled haunches, dusty mer-
cantile center where one of Quanah's wives, Tonarcy, purchased
a corset to wear to Theodore Roosevelt's inauguration, which
she at first wore outside the dress.

No close-huddled enclave, however sociable, can shut out the
utterly silent fearsomeness of these high open plains. The echoes
of whoops and death screams, eagles' cries and coyotes' laughter,
have died out. Now the only sounds that waft through the wind are
on radio waves. For the people of the little towns, they are like
waves of refreshing rain against the drought of the spirit, a less
perfidious rain than that dark swatch which hangs in the air in

West Texas, but never quite reaches the ground. In the little towns they wake up and bed down to the music. Boys still walk on tin-can stilts and girls cut out old Sears catalog paper dolls to the music. Barbers barber and dogs howl to it. This music is for the fresh and ruddy, rough and ready, tough and rutty. For the grit and his girl. The sounds connect one overloaded heart to another. The hearts must huddle or die of loneliness.

It is barely dawn and already the wind is kicking up the dust. It was sending empty beer cans skittering across the parking lot when he came to the station. Spooky. Nowhere but Texas. Nowhere so constant a wind as in Texas, grating like Willie Nelson's voice, like memory's three-sided rasp working across his heart. Three grades of abrasion: coarse, medium, and fine, across the grain. He flips off his mike and groans. Only one besides Willie Nelson who could make him feel near as bad was Patsy Cline. The swivel chair squeaks its own mournful sprung sound as he rolls his bulk around, chasing the scraps of paper that constitute his script. He remembers the winds of his life. Looking at a tornado coming. Standing in the road and looking at it, pardner. The blended smell of urine and cowdung blown in strongly from the feedlot. You smell it in your coffee cup in the mornings. Trash and grit blowing in the streets. You develop a lifetime squint. It's not the sun that makes you squint. It's the wind. Squeezes out the tears, then dries 'em right off, before you know why you were crying in the first place.

She was a redhead. They're all alike. There must be something about red hair that seeps down into the brain, reckon? He suspicioned she was running around on him. And it turned out true. It was happening while he had the late shift at the station. Now he was on days and she was long gone to Dallas. Now he goes by himself to the feed-ins at Junior's on Friday night, where they'd had some fun. Or sits with the TV on, drinking from a case of beer stashed in the icebox, taking out his Fender six-string guitar night after night and picking at it for hours at a time. Besides his guitar, there is nothing left but this job, which he is kicking over today. The job, he realizes, had kept him sane and sober enough to roll out every morning before dawn. He looks down at his beer belly. It's coming right along. He has a lot of listeners, good friends, out there, who've known him all the forty years of his life. But nobody real close to him, if you didn't count Zula Staggs, night waitress at the last cafe going out of town.

"Aw, mercy, mercy, now, that's Willie Nelson, talkin' awhile, sangin' awhile...."

Maybe he was a sorry so-and-so. All hat and no cattle. That's Charlie. But she even quit keeping Christmas. Wasn't any use with just the two of them, she said. Too expensive. Too much trouble. Made him mad as hell. Anything he tried to do she took the contrary side. After she left he would have plain kicked off without his guitar. Ohhhhh, lonesome me. Lonesome as one dove on a telephone wire. Today he is going to sell the guitar and get out of Floydada for good.

"Big Charlie spinning that country sound your way until eleven this morning."

Saturday morning. Her fingers turn the dial, seemingly of their own volition.

"Aw, mercy, mercy, now, that's Willie Nelson, talkin' awhile, sangin' awhile. Ever' thang alright out there? KKAP Voice of the Caprock Floydada Texas, little darlin'. Six-oh-five A.M. Big Charlie spinning that country sound your way until eleven this morning.

"Lo-retta Lynn's gonna start it off this mornin'. Gonna sang 'When the Tangle Becomes a Chill.' Sang it, Lo-retta."

She had been a month in the "Little House on the Prairie"— what she called her grasshopper-green stucco perched on a dusty, wind-blown plot at the edge of town. She was the new teacher in town, "hired-on" after the break-up of her marriage to Jack Hammer, a peripatetic oil man she had met at Mardi Gras. Strange convolutions of chemistry, youthful blindness, and cruel fate led them to marry and traverse Texas several times before

landing in Floydada, from which she refused to budge when Jack
made his final departure for richer oil fields. He was gallant to
the end. "Me and Sweet Thang just got crosswise" was all he
would say about their break-up.

So here she was, French Catholic from New Orleans, playing
her prized classical tapes at decibels that shook the stucco walls,
concentrating on what she would teach on Monday to stay one
step, or even a half-step ahead of her class—this is the way she
kept her sanity.

Floydada. Not dada as in dada art, but long *a*, as in "hate 'er."
The name hadn't the graphic literalness of, for example, Plainview,
Tx. (where, incidentally, they had also lived), but Floydada
conveyed a definite dreary subliminal message all its own.

"Lawd a mercy, that's beautiful, honey. Gonna take a little
tour now with 'My Honky Tonk Heart.'" The singer chews his
words casually and spits them in a brown stream against the
microphone. Throughout the flat dry morning the wagon train
rolls on to some back-home golden spread where the hootch is
the hootchiest, rubes are the rubiest, boobs are the boobiest, all
to the sound of yodeling, the catch in the throat, the crack in the
voice, the tired voice, the nasal inflection; in men, the whiskey
voice, the old voice, talking the lyrics; in women, the flint-hard
voice disguised under soft martyred tones.

"Aw, sang it now, angel. Gonna cut out now for the market
report, but I'll be back 'fore you can say Englebert Humperdinck,
hee-hee-hee, so don't go away. Stay tuned to Ol' Charlie here.
Here's Arvel Sprayberry with the U.S. Department of Ag-
gerculture's latest market reports."

She tried to tune out Arvel Sprayberry, but her little house
needed sound inside. Her little house, with its gray composition
roof, still had Xmas lights strung across the eaves of the porch,
though it was now mid-February. On the sparse brown stubble
of grass in the yard there were even a few strands of once-festive
tinsel caught here and there, determined to add their cheerless
touch. They hung on desperately, just as the prickly stuff to
which they were attached clung tight to keep the whole dirt yard

from blowing away. At the side of the house, leaning on skinny legs against a window, an evaporative cooler rested its trunk and relived painful old summer memories in red rust streaks down the grasshopper-green wall. But even ghastly green was better than white, because white quickly collects the dust and becomes brown.

"Trade very slow in the Panhandle area today," muttered Arvel tensely through clenched teeth and immobile lips. "Steers trading 59-59-50 this morning. Choice heifers 56-56-50. Cattle quotations for slaughter cows, cutter, and boning utility unavailable. Choice steer carcasses 59 and steady." The soporific drone would put anyone to sleep, even those steers and heifers whose imminent demise it forecast.

Big Charlie's hearty voice boomed in, reassuringly, "Arvel, yur as nervous as a long-tail cat in a room full of rockin' chairs. Git on back to yur computer, thar, Arvel."

There had been an unexpected vacancy in the high school for the second semester. The school principal, Stilson M. Rench, had mercifully been very busy on the January day he interviewed her.

"Why do you want to work in our community, Judy?"

She wanted to say, "Because I like to eat," but she stammered something about introducing youngsters to the worlds of biology and English literature, expanding their universe, and so on, and then could have kicked herself all over Texas for not telling him what he wanted to hear: that she would enthusiastically sell popcorn for band uniforms, chaperon proms, intrepidly police both boys' and girls' bathrooms, teach Sunday School, and file absence slips in the office on her lunch break.

Throughout the interview she prayed, "Please don't ask about evolution, please don't ask about evolution." At this point in her downward spiral, if he had asked, "Judy, do you believe that the world is round or flat?" she would have declared, "I can teach it either way."

She continued to pray, "Don't ask my religion. Don't ask my religion."

"What...," he began.

She held her breath.

"...do you think of our nifty football record last season?"

"Nifty!" she breathed.

She was hired on.

"Turkey in the Straw" struts forth from the radio. Damn! Is this kazoo-and-washboard piece the only background music KKAP has for commercials? They use it to sell everything from fertilizer to fashions.

"...Seriously, folks, when you are lookin' for real down-to-arth savings on yur family clothing needs, there ain't no place you'll do aaaaaany better than our own Double T Ranch Store. [Down music.] Yessir, home-owned and operated, where you'll find the lowest pra-ces and the fa-nest quality in men, women, and kiddos' western wire, so come on down and visit with our friendly, alert, and qualified personnel today at Double T Ranch Wire. [Up "Turkey in the Straw."]

"Young 'uns, last night I had the chicken-fried steak of my dreams out at Junior's Steak House. Love their chicken-fried steak, biscuits, and watt gravy. And I can fairly *graze* at that salad bar. Don't fergit the Friday night buffet. Your mouth will go crazy. All you can eat for one low pras.... You can eat and eat and eat...and eat...and eat...[Echo chamber, fading out.] Junior's Steak House. Remember Junior's for your dining pleasure. Your mouth will thank you. Highway 82 and Farm-to-Market 1171. Tell 'em Big Charlie sent you.

"Remember, Jeannine Teakell'll be comin' on at eleven with the Country Tradin' Post—the Garage Sale of the Ire—so call in yur items to her at 717-0025."

More music. Metaphor is mixed in an Osterizer and poured out unashamedly: "Ever' time you cross my mind, you break my heart." The morning whines away. She vows she will work her way out of this place as fast as her Louisiana legs will take her. But she is committed to teach for the rest of this year. How will she bear it? Maybe with Mahler. Yes.

Now for some Saturday-morning Mahler.

"...the One and the Only Patsy Cline, sangin' 'Leavin' on Your Mind.'"

Oh, Big Charlie. Why did you have to play that one? It's one of the great truth-telling country songs. That kind of raunchy truth, born of great pain, keeps me listening to you. Charlie, I guess whenever I've got the lovesick blues, I'll have to turn off Mahler and turn on—you. You are just a voice in the wind, but I feel like huddling in your arms.

"Well, folks, it's been real nas playin' yur favorites this mornin'. Time for yours truly to slide on out. Stay tuned for Jeannine Teakell and the Country Tradin' Post, and then Olney Forbes gon' set with you 'til five o'clock, playing more of yur good ol' country sounds off the top of the chart. Lawd, Jeannine, I'm runnin' over. Got to bail out of here, girl, I got dirt to scratch and eggs to lay." Off-mike, he grabs Jeannine's arm. "Honey, be sure to ask if anybody wants to buy my six-string guitar. I got a dandy one for sale. Mother of pearl inlaid." He switches the mike back on for her with a Big Charlie guffaw. "See ya later, Floydada!"

She doesn't want to hear Mahler. Or even Beethoven. She starts to change the station but what else can she get except KZZZ Crosbyton or KDOO McAdoo?

The radio again breaks into her thoughts. "...party has a pire of watt cheers upholstered in genuine naugahyde...."

That's it! She feels a little lift. She never thought she would be Saturday-morning-happy again, especially here in this dusty corner of the world, feeling a bit of grit between her teeth as she swallows hard, picks up the telephone.

She dials the number.

"Hello, Jeannine? This is Judy Hammer, 717-4392. Yes, I'm fine. How are *yew*? Jeannine, would you please give out my number over the air for anyone who has a western guitar he wants to sell?"

Beyond Telling

A pity beyond all telling
Is hid in the heart of love:
The folk who are buying and selling,
The clouds on their journey above,
The cold wet winds ever blowing,
And the shadowy hazel grove
Where mouse-grey waters are flowing,
Threaten the head that I love.
—W. B. Yeats

The floating rib of the moon had snagged on the humid, black, almost visceral, folds of a Louisiana summer night. There it lodged, a bright bone detained for a few hours above white suburbs and the black low-pitched roofs of Golden Gardens, Inc.

Inside, supper had been stomached, and now Prospère Pataud's jam box grudgingly reproduced big band sounds from his table near the front door, where he habitually hung out on Saturday nights with his coffee and cigarettes, hawking everyone who came or went. Called Gumbo, victim of the French propensity to nickname everyone, he was the only one in the place with eyes that seemed to expect something to happen momentarily. They were not happy eyes, however; set deep in the walnut puckers of his face, they were black, half-lidded, as if the thing that he expected might not be pleasant.

In the southeast quadrant of the lobby, where a snaggle-toothed piano leaned against a wall, the still-ambulatory fidgeted. An old man dry as a stick hobbled to an alleged destination, shifting his genitals gingerly as he went, a habitual gesture, shifting them gently, doting on them. From her rocker Grammaw Modeste scolded an empty chair at her right hand, the wild frizz on her head like horsehair escaped from an old davenport. Subsiding into silence, she rocked smartly for a while. Then she turned to her left, where a woman with spavined ankles sat in a wheelchair with her hands in her lap, one hand upturned in the palm of the other. "Was it you died or your sister?"

The second woman's mouth was permanently puckered up to one side as by a faulty drawstring. "It was my sister," she mumbled.

"Then, who are you?"

"Don't you know who I am?"

"No, but you go up to that desk in the hall. They can tell you who you are."

Heaped all together, these about-to-be-dead continued to segregate themselves by race, and secondarily by sex, as though some irreparable harm might result from their close proximity. Like crippled survivors of a night-marauder, like fowl in the corner of a slaughterhouse awaiting the ax, they huddled with their own. Ghosts of the safely dead floated restlessly around the music, courting the halt, the blind, and the immobile, choosing partners for the next dance.

In the back of the facility a less-prescient group, the all-but-dead, were lying quietly not caring. They could be called the less fortunate, or the more fortunate, according to how you look at things.

A tall, gray-haired black man with a newspaper under his arm left his group across the large lobby, which doubled as a dining area at mealtime, and approached Gumbo's table, walking briskly but mechanically. Gumbo grasped his propped-up hand crutches and put them deliberately across the seat of the other chair at his table.

"Good evenin', Mr. Gumbo."

"Evenin', U.U."

U.U. coolly drew up a third chair from an adjacent table. He tossed the newspaper on the table and draped himself over the straight chair, one arm flung limply and companionably over the back of it, one long leg crossed over the other with so much leg left over, it hung out in space.

That was the man all over, thought Gumbo. Pushy.

"Nice music," said the man.

"Oh, hell yeah, man! It's the only music worth a damn today. And it ain't easy to fine, no. I found me a station in Baton Rouge—WGGZ-FM. 98.1. They play it 'til ten o'clock at night and then they sign off."

"But you don't go to bed then." He was expressing a truism of the place. In contrast to most of the residents, who slept concretely as effigies, diurnally, nocturnally, datelessly, Gumbo seldom rumpled his bed. He roamed.

"No, I don't sleep much, me. Tonight they sign off at midnight since it's Saddy. Oh, boy, I love Saddy nights!" A fixed, limp cigarette in the corner of his mouth—it looked recycled—glowingly resuscitated as he drew in, listening. "Hot damn! Artie Shaw. Did you used to dance much, U.U.?"

"I don't know how to dance."

But they dance out of the womb. A nigger that didn't dance. That's something. He was a good looking old buck, too. "Man, I had your legs I'd be dancing at the Kit Kat Club every night."

"Hee-hee-heee." U.U.'s chuckle was saying hee-hee-hee, but it was deep and rolling. Gumbo laughed with him. U.U. was all right. He was a classy nigger. He had been principal of Carver High before it was closed for integration, but his heart was so bad, he had come down with pneumonia six or eight times. Finally he just moved in here for perpetual care since his wife was dead.

Gumbo sighed. He thought about his own dead wife. He stared in his coffee cup, swallowed from it autohypnotically. He drew on the cigarette butt, then made a tiny accordion of it in the ashtray.

U.U. read his newspaper. He had been born into a preacher's family and he himself had preached some. He was educated at Southern University, took a master's degree at Normal, Illinois, and other postgraduate work at two other northern schools: Harvard and Columbia. His wife Selena had been handsome, from the plantation. She was not educated, but she had been a strong woman, a dignified woman. She had been a good wife and mother. They had much in common. But they couldn't sit and talk about books or ideas. Their children now lived in Los Angeles, Philadelphia, and Atlanta.

"Hmm. Hmmm. Umph-umph," he said. He was hoping to nudge a little interest from Gumbo. "Look here what's coming out of Washington now."

"Nahh." Gumbo jerked his head sideways in disgust, dismissed the whole subject. "Politicians. We ain't had a man for all the people since ol' Huey Long." He didn't like politics. There wasn't any fun in it. He jerked up straight, seeing a woman in a wheelchair steering her way determinedly across the floor. "Oh, here she come, 'round the mountain," he said gleefully. "Hey, Miss Nessa, over here! Over here!" One more tough lady.

He nudged U.U. "Miss Nessa. She came last week. She's one more. Maybe you know her. She used to teach school, but you were probably before her time," he added ungenerously, purposely.

"Oh, yes, I do remember Miss Vanessa. Vanessa Derbigny. Well, do. I sure do remember her. Hee-Hee-Hee."

"Is she a pistol. Lots of pain in her legs. Told me one day her little grandniece Millie asked her what she would do without her leg. That was when she was threatening to lose one of her legs from diabetes and phlebitis. Told Millie she'd use a crutch. And Millie asked, like kids do, what would she do if they cut the other leg off? Miss Nessa said, 'I'd push myself around on a scooter.' Then Millie said, What if they cut your arms off. 'I'd learn to live as a torso,' she told her. What's a torso?—smart little TeeDeets, that child—and Nessa had to explain what a torso was. I guarantee, Nessa would have made the best of it—if she had to, she would have been the best damn torso she could be.

"What the hell! She's stopping to talk to somebody. —Hey,

Miss Nessa! She got a laugh out of it when I first met her, I told her my joke about myself. 'Yeah,' I said, real cool, 'I'm in here with my mother-in-law.' I'm flicking my cigarette and I'm taking a big slug of coffee while she fields that one. 'Yeah!' I said. 'What the hell are you doing,' I said to them, 'putting my mother-in-law in here!' Can you beat that? My wife died and I end up in here with HER. 'Yeah, Modeste, that's the one,' I said, 'that one you hear screaming and cursing every morning at 4 A.M. Screams right through breakfast.' They say she don't know me. She knows me, I guarantee. Goddams me every time she lays eyes on me. I just tell her, 'Go in your room, old woman, ten' to your crochet!' Sure, I avoid her. But she's here. You know? She's here in the place. God, U.U., I wish I had my wife back. Somebody to bitch to."

U.U. was staring at the lady. Gumbo stopped for a breath and to wait for U.U.'s "Heee," which didn't come, so he continued, "After I met Miss Nessa I gave her a big crucifix my wife used to have in the bedroom. I made her a present of it and was she tickled. She said she would always keep it under her pillow. And you know what? When I check on her at night, she's always sleeping propped up, hugging it up on her buzooms like a little dolly.

"She has to use a wheelchair a lot to keep her legs elevated. She's learning how to get around, though. Her eyes went bad, too, from the diabetes. You don't need eyes in this place. You get to know it like the palm of your hand. Hey, Miss Nessa! Boy, oh boy! There's nothing I wouldn't do for that woman."

"You haven't got any legs either." U.U. halted the flow. It didn't come out like he meant it to. "At least, I mean...hell, they're there, but not of much use to you."

"Yeah, but I'm a man. Here she come— Hey, Miss Nessa."

"Hey, Prospère." She peered at him through thick lenses. Her disease had just about ruined her vision, but had spared her face, a face beloved by generations of schoolkids. She had extraordinarily fine skin, French-knotted black hair, lots of gray in it, and a quick, broad, white smile. She wheeled closer. A bright flowered print dress covered to the ankles her bound legs.

Gumbo noted that his station was playing "In the Mood." Original Glenn Miller band. Just the right thing. Later on, maybe, "Stardust." She was stardust. She was string of pearls and Tuxedo Junction. Gumbo fantasized himself in a tux taking her out to the floor, all that black hair would be tumbled down, not pinned up, his hand would be lightly guiding her in the small of her back, resting lightly in that hair.

U.U. stood up. Gumbo struggled to his feet. She allowed them to. U.U. liked that. Pain grabbed his heart. To see her debilitated like this was a terrible shock. He wanted to say this to her but he couldn't talk. Maybe she didn't even remember him. Should he introduce himself? She looked almost the same as the last time he had glimpsed her, seemingly years ago. She stood up for blacks, he remembered. She had been educated up north, too. Their paths had seldom crossed except at citywide teachers' meetings. She always walked young.

Gumbo remained standing, leaning on his crutches while she drew near the table, fighting the wheelchair, not yet adroit enough to get in close. U.U. moved her in closer until the flowered skirt was well hidden beneath the table.

"I'm gon' get you some coffee," Gumbo declared.

U.U. jerked around. "I'll get it, Prospère," he said, but Gumbo was already gone, scuttling on his hand sticks over to the small rolling cart that held the coffee urn.

"I'm Vanessa Derbigny, Mr. Lumière."

"Lord, yes," rolling out his deep heeee and shaking his head side to side in the grip of grief and joy, "Miss Vanessa. You in this place. Lord. Lord."

"Yes. Well. I've been here only a week. Someone told me you were here. Why are you here?"

"I've been here seven years. I must have broken a mirror."

He used to have dimples, she thought. Killer dimples, the less inhibited female teachers had called them. They had elongated into laugh lines, or maybe age lines, around his mouth. "You've been retired—?"

"Eight years. My heart is too bad to make it on my own. I keep on getting pneumonia."

"The same thing happened to me." *Missed the Saturday dance.* "I mean, I got very sick as soon as I retired. I have diabetes and thrombophlebitis in this leg. I've had diabetes for twenty-five years. It got bad and so did the phlebitis during my last year of teaching and I suffered through it." *Heard they crowded the floor.* "I've been here a week."

"Welcome."

"Yesterday I went back to the house to settle things. Linda, my niece, and her husband Hap and Little Millie—she's my grand-niece—took me there in their car and Millie wheeled me around the place in a collapsible wheelchair. And I settled the business of the house and...things...in the house. They are going to pick everything they want before I sell the rest. Hap was immensely helpful with all the details of selling the house and whatever chattel was left. They are my only living relations. Half the town promised to visit, however. Some really have, my teacher friends, neighbors, and people from St. Michael-St. Gabriel. Even some of my students, who are middle-aged now, can you imagine? Yes, you can imagine, can't you? But Linda's been my mainstay, coming every day this week with little Millie, bless her."

"I hope you like it black." Gumbo had come back with a mug of coffee held by a forefinger and thumb while still handling his crutches, and he had proudly set it down in front of Vanessa. "Hey, U.U., we like our coffee like our women, *hein?* Strong, hot, and black." He was suddenly embarrassed by what he had said. "Hey, man, I didn't get you any coffee. I can't carry two, anyway."

"It's alright, I don't want any."

"Prospère Pataud!" She was mortified by what Gumbo had said. She smoothed it over quickly, hating her hypocrisy as she ladled it over the three of them. "Prospère's been showing me around all week. He sort of attached himself to me on the first day. Remember Skippy Doane, Mr. Lumière, who became the

big football star? Prospère reminded me of Skippy on my first
day of teaching in junior high. Skippy showed me the ropes,
related the latest atrocities, and read me the Gospel according to
the Eighth Grade. And Prospère did the same. He was like a
lifeline for me when I first came here."

"Did he warn you about Mouche yet?"

"Oh—Mouche! Yes! I found out about her for myself. She has
had to jab me a few times. She's not nice."

"Tough as a boiled owl," said Gumbo. "Meaner woman never
lived, U.U. Meaner woman never lived."

"She walks like she's pulling a load," laughed U.U.

"Man, her dress moving one way, and she moving the other."
Ashes dropped from Gumbo's cigarette as he talked.

"Hee-Heee! She has a muzzle full of whisker-holes, but no
whiskers!"

"She have to be satisfied with her mustache."

"Cut it out, you two!" Vanessa gave them her broad white
smile. "But listen: She has ulcers and can't stop smoking and
eating everything that's bad for her. Her son is gay, her husband
is an alcoholic, all the family members labeled something, you
know? She has one of everything—"

U.U. thought, *She's also racist. That's her label.*

"—so I forgive her for being so mean."

Got as far as the door issued from the radio. She had mentally
detached as Millie had wheeled her through the house. Goodbye
tester bed, goodbye stove, goodbye rolltop desk, goodbye house
and porch. The wind's rocking in my rocker now.

But no more worries now. No burglars, no rapists, no falling
down my steps. No steps. No more aluminum siding salesmen,
bogus roofers, thousand-dollar radiation monitors with mainte-
nance contracts, handy men and handy boys to steal your tools,
neighbor boys to steal your pecans, no pecan trees, no boys at all,
no children, no neighbors— *But why stir up memories?* She
glanced at U.U. "What is that song they're playing? Oh, yes.
'Don't Get Around Much Anymore.'"

"Look, Miss Nessa." Gumbo pointed to the front door.

"—Well, here's Linda and Millie!"

The little girl ran up to her. "Nana! Nana!" She wore a pastel flowered dress with a big white lace collar, white leggings and black patent shoes. Her mother followed, looking like a grown-up version of Millie, except that her black patent heels spiked the floor mercilessly. She wore white hose, a flowered dress with a linen collar, and pearl-like beads around her neck, matching earrings. She carried a very smart, large black patent handbag with an oversized pearlized clasp.

"Nana!" Linda embraced Vanessa and Millie together, wrapped the patent leather purse around them protectively. "You look so good, dawlin', how are you feeling? Did the doctor see you today? He is supposed to see you once a week at the first. You let me know if he doesn't. Is the food O.K.? Francie is making shrimp and corn soup tomorrow and I'll bring you some. Do I need to take out the shrimp?" And, talking without awaiting a reply, she wheeled her aunt away to another area of the lobby. Gumbo and U.U. watched them, watched Millie climb confidently onto Vanessa's lap, chattering and pulling various indispensable items out of her tiny purse.

"We can't compete with that, *hein*?" Gumbo nestled over his radio.

"No indeed," laughed U.U. "Sure can't."

Vanessa's kin visited for an hour by the clock. Millie joined a bingo game that was getting under way. She played, sitting on Vanessa's lap, until she won a hot dog, then lost interest when her mother wouldn't let her eat it.

"Well, Nana, it must be getting near your bedtime!" exclaimed Linda when the hour was up. "I know *somebody* here who is getting sleepy!"

"Not me," said Millie, but allowed herself to be taken away. She and her mother waved and waved, and Vanessa waved them out of sight.

When his station went off the air at midnight, Gumbo slung his jam box over his shoulder by its strap, and left Vanessa and U.U. All they were talking was teacher-business, anyway. It was boring. He told them he needed to check on his kids. The nurses in the juvenile unit let him go through at odd hours during the night. He could be very quiet when he wanted to. He liked to watch them sleep. If anyone of them was restless, he soothed him. Many of them were bedfast, some dependent on oxygen monitored digitally second by second. Some of the kids had large bellies. Except for the young adults and adult-retarded, all were in heartbreakingly small white-painted hospital beds, iron cages. Their rooms were a poor kid's dream, filled floor to ceiling and wall to wall with Disney characters both three-dimensional and flat, balloons and autographed pennants, heaps of the most lovable of all Gund creations, picture books, games, color TV's, posters, and exquisite, perfect dolls.

U.U. and Vanessa talked on until two in the morning. She was hungry for talk. They discussed loneliness, and at the end of that topic, both realized without saying it, that they were not so lonely now.

She said, "I used to try to get my kids to think. I used to throw out the question: 'What is hell?' Got some wildly funny answers."

"And what is hell?"

"It's your own grand hotel on the Riviera, totally unpopulated. 'Think about it,' I used to tell them."

She caved in suddenly at two. U.U. rolled her over to the vending area in the children's day room, bought her an apple and a diet drink from the phalanx of machines against the wall.

"You know, I've never seen Gumbo eat anything," she said.

"He lives on coffee and cigarettes. He may be nurtured by a vending machine. He hangs out here with the kids a lot."

"Gumbo's tastebuds are right on target. The food here. What can I say about it? The food here is masticable. There is plenty of it."

"Heeee!" He shook his head delightedly. "Here we are in a community of world-class cooks and cut off from some of the best cooking in the world. What a shame."

"Yes, food is such a solace."

"But old people are like children, they generally don't pay much attention to what they eat. Meals are only something you get through. You must have it rougher since you are a diabetic."

"It's really all the same. Every day the food smells the same, although I must say the proper food groups are represented. Stuff that resembles dairy products, fibers, withered leaves, tubulars, lumps that might be fruits, protein slabs, legumes, fat, starches, and liquids, all bound together by artificial flavors and sweeteners...."

"You're right. It smells all the same. It doesn't smell good or bad, but institutional. Not hot and not cold by the time we get it, not colored, not uncolored, sort of a uniform gray, but better, I reckon, than artificial colors."

"And the noise!"

"It's better than silence."

"I'm gradually getting used to it, except when the aides try to outshout the residents. Prospère's mother-in-law..."

"Modeste! What a pair of lungs."

"Then there are the smells," she said.

"I don't smell anything anymore."

"It smells...kind of sick...sometimes. But so does a house sometimes, *n'est-çe pas?* I think I have been cursed with a stronger sense of smell and taste while my other senses are deteriorating."

He rolled her back to her room, past Mouche nodding at the nurses' station, and rang for an aide to help her. While they waited, a long time, he turned back the gray sheets on her bed and put the head of the bed up high, the way she said she liked it. It gave her a feeling of better control over her environment, she said. When the aide came, U.U. said goodnight rather suddenly and disappeared. She lay, or rather, sat up in bed with Gumbo's crucifix on her breast and went immediately to sleep. It was the first night she had not sat up staring for hours at her swollen legs in the moonlight before dropping off into nightmarish dreams. She did not hear Modeste's screams this night. Mouche plunged into her room at 5 A.M. to administer her insulin injection. "I'm perfectly able to inject myself," Vanessa objected. "I've been doing it all my life."

"No ma'am," Mouche said firmly. "We do not self-medicate in here."

She didn't argue. She didn't have a place to refrigerate the insulin anyway. Sitting up very contentedly in bed, she soon fell back deeply asleep.

They told their life stories in the following days, closely shadowed by Pataud. Sometimes Gumbo wore a paper surgical mask with a hole cut in the middle for his cigarette. Or he dribbled a small stream of ketchup from the corner of his mouth to simulate blood. It invited comment and warded off boredom. Today he was wearing a red toothbrush behind his ear.

U.U. acknowledged the toothbrush with a genial "Heeeee" and turned to "his ladyfriend," as Gumbo called her.

"Were you ever married, Miss Nessa?"

"No."

"I didn't know for sure because every Southern lady is a Miss. She could have three husbands and twelve children, but she still is a Miss. It's some kind of deferential mark after she attains a certain age, isn't it?"

"Well, I'm not ashamed to be Miss Nessa and I'm not ashamed of being sixty-seven."

"I'm sixty-six, me," said Gumbo. "I got in here on Medicaid."

Vanessa reminisced to U.U. "I remember what you did for your kids." She glanced at his long, long legs. When he walked the campus it was *drama*. "Your kids said you were never in your office, you paced the halls—"

"—Snooped around!"

"Like me!" put in Gumbo. The red toothbrush slipped from his ear and fell with a *tic* to the table.

"—just impatient to know every day's achievement, small though it might be. You pushed them, not in a mean way, but by showing them how to believe in themselves."

"I don't know. I had to turn them over to others in the end. But others have taken up the work."

"That must have hurt some."

"When we integrated and I moved to the new school, there was one thing that really hurt: the callous way they destroyed the identity of old Carver High. It meant nothing to them. We had a case of athletic and academic trophies in the main hall. They took out the trophies and did away with them. We don't know to this day what happened to them. I think they just pitched them. It meant nothing to them."

"Shameful. Awful. You must be very bitter about that."

"I was. Now I am just sad when I think about it. I haven't thought about it in years."

She told him what teaching had meant to her. In spite of all the disappointments, the bad apples, the clashes with administrators and parents—outside of all that, standing on their own, there were the kids. "The kids never really disappointed me." Not even the toughest ones, those hard, stubborn little buds so tightly furled in her hands for so long. No wonder she pressed their blossoms in her memory book. "The thinking of the young, their thought processes, are so intense, it was a joy to follow them." She sighed.

Gumbo said, "Don't pine too much for the old days, Miss Nessa."

U.U. said, "Don't worry about life on the outside. There is no life out there for us."

She was listening, her chin resting in her palms. She looked at his face questioningly but he was dead serious, lowering his brows at her behind his steel rims. "It's not real out there. Real life is here. This is the center of our lives now."

"Golden Gardens? It's true, I guess. I'm not at home out there anymore. I feel it already after just a few weeks."

"Not only that." He searched for the words. "I don't know how to describe it here. It's like the Garden of Eden in reverse. Full of innocent children, but all the similarities to childhood are a cruel joke." He looked embarrassed momentarily, then continued, "But this place is the real world—not outside. Men, women, and children are suffering. There is more desperate, intense life going on here than outside."

"You think, then, that all this pain lifts us up?"

"Surely, surely. Great adventures are taking place here. Epic deeds. To get up and dress yourself!"

She thought that she would marry the man if he asked her at this moment.

"Lawd have mussy!" said Gumbo. "Sounds to me like you are describing a concentration camp."

"Right!" U.U. leaned forward. "Why do you think a concentration camp was so named? It was a point of concentration for the undesirables in the population. It so happened that the undesirables were the good and the 'genetically superior' were the evil. Same as here. There is so much good here. There is so much evil. It shocks you when you come up on it, like stumbling onto the Grand Canyon."

It had been a long time since he had preached like that. He was angry with himself and embarrassed. He had crossed some kind of line with her and they both knew it.

"Jesus Christ," said Gumbo. "Sit and listen to this I might as well be in a church." He left them—he felt snubbed; besides, he saw his mother-in-law coming.

U.U. apologized for spouting off.

"No! Don't ever apologize for what is the best part of you!" But they were mannered and forced with one another for the rest of the day.

In the evening he brought her to her room, summoned an aide, and turned to leave. She caught his hand. "Thanks."

"Oh, yes," he said shyly. Slowly, as in a dream, he moved closer. He couldn't help himself. He took her head in his hands and held it, loving her, afraid for her. Her health was so fragile. She was so intelligent, *was* intelligence. She put her hands around his hands.

In a few short weeks, it was readily apparent to every resident or nurse who was not slack-jawed and snoring that Vanessa Derbigny and U.U. Lumière were "a pair."

Gumbo hid his feelings generally, but he opened up to Mouche. "Much as I liked her; yeah, I really really liked that woman, but much as I liked her, that was something out of the blue, I guarantee...that way she is about niggers...what she is trying to pull off with him. It ain't right. It just ain't right and wouldn't be right in ten thousand years. I called her a lady and she was. But I can't forgive her for what she is doing. Hell, I don't know what she is doing. What they are doing. How should I know? But I can't forgive her. I don't know if I ever could. Damn! I wish my wife was here. She would have plenty to say about that! I guarantee!" Mouche took his words verbatim and added choice observations of her own for the night shift.

In point of fact, they were planning to get married. No one knew this, not even Gumbo, although he could have guessed it because, among other things, U.U. wheeled her around the grounds every day at sundown and their faces showed it when they came back indoors. They also went out at night to watch the phases of the moon, joining all past humankind out wanting under the stars. They laughed at everything and they always ate together. But Gumbo only spied on them from afar. He stayed strictly away from them now.

One evening when Venus was swinging earthward, pendant from the moon on a black velvet cord, Vanessa had proposed. "I want to marry you," she said.

He wanted to, oh, yes, he wanted to, but he refused at first. "Oh, no, Miss Nessa, my dear Nessa. I wouldn't do this to you."

"I love you. I love you so...wildly...that if I had the legs I would go run off a cliff—if we had a cliff. Can you imagine that kind of despair. And happiness. I've ransacked heaven and earth looking for you. I waited a lifetime for you. I want to marry you. Am I crazy?"

Her voice was singing in his ears. Oh, ears. Are you appreciating what she is saying? "My love," she was saying. "My only help this side of sanity. Aren't you going to read the Song of Solomon to me? I want you to read to me every night. If we're married we can share a room."

"I want to read to you. I want to be with you when you can't sleep, do all the little things for you that the aides don't do or won't. I want to pray with you."

"Then marry me."

Such a little step. Across a threshold. Take it. "I will. I will."

"So will I." They would place her in heaven with those who were insane on earth. It's all right by me. That's the place for me. Vanessa at sixteen would not have believed these facts. A severe diabetic, unmarried until the age of 67, then married, to a Negro in a nursing home. Poor girl. She would have thrown herself off the Mississippi River Bridge.

I will have his name. Will I be buried in the white cemetery or the black? Is it possible this is happening to me? The follies of our youth! What about the follies of our old age? What is it nagging me? I can defy everybody. I don't care what they think. The only one nagging me is Linda. Not Hap. Not little Millie. It's Linda.

Linda seemed to become ill when her aunt told her. She had trouble standing on her spiked heels. Her face looked like an egg that had been taken out of cold storage and was now sweating at room temperature. She wobbled drunkenly to a chair, crying copiously. Once seated in the chair, she recovered, her adrenalin was redirected and she was positively outraged.

Vanessa met her squarely. "Linda, he treats me reverentially, but like an equal. Something no white man, especially a principal, ever did."

"Treats you like an equal! What are you talking about?" She groped for more ammunition. "Hap and I will just have you moved to another health care facility."

"Not without my permission."

While Linda carried on, Vanessa concentrated on Modeste's ravings down the hall. She was screaming through her breakfast.

It was soothing to Vanessa to hear the familiar epithets. She was home. She stood her ground and let Linda rage about Vanessa's place in the community, what she was doing to their family, that they were people used to something and people used to something just don't do that. Even poor whites don't associate with Negroes! Much less marry them!

"I'm not in Louisiana, Linda. I am free for the first time in my life to do what I want to do. This concentration camp has freed me."

"Not in Louisiana! You are talking completely out of your head. Are you crazy or what? Yes, you've always been a little bit crazy. Like that time you went to Stranger Home Church. To listen to James Farmer! The police saw you there."

"Linda, that was thirty years ago!"

"—People saw you there!"

"And I wish to this day I had marched with them!"

"—I could live that down. But, this! U.U. Lumière! He is just a low-down con artist trying to get into your money. He thinks you have more money than you do. He is an uppity... arrogant... Negro!" He always has been. But why do I have to tell you, a sixty-something old lady, all this? To marry a Negro! Are you senile? No, nobody gets that senile! Well, I have my pride. And my daughter's future to think about. I'll tell you what, I am going to tell everybody you are senile. It's the only way I can take all this. And since you are senile there's no point in visiting you."

"Let me show you the way out," said Vanessa.

When he tried to pull the details of the scene out of her, she would tell him only that Linda had broken off with her. "I will miss seeing Millie grow up. But then, I won't be around long enough for that anyway." She shook off the thought. "Millie will remember how I loved her. She will know the truth one day."

"Yes. She's very perceptive. When she matures, she'll understand. She will marvel at us someday."

"Meanwhile, she'll forget Nana's name."

They made their plans. They joked about their religious

differences. "Oh, I couldn't possibly marry outside the church," she said. He broke up with laughter. He was a Baptist. "O.K., Nessa. O.K." He stomped his foot, shook his head, bending over with laughter.

"I have it all planned. I'll get a New Orleans priest. They've seen everything." She wrote one of her former students, Father John Passy, stationed in New Orleans, explaining their relationship, how perfect it was. She asked if he would come up to Plancher-des-Vaches and marry them. U.U. wanted just a few hours' instruction in the Catholic faith, she wrote, he was already an ordained minister.

"You know that we will be segregated in death," U.U. said to her.

"I already have a plot in the Catholic cemetery. But I will sell it and get one wherever it is that you will be buried."

"No, I won't have you in the black cemetery. You belong in the white Catholic cemetery."

"I belong to you. We'll buy a plot close to mine for you in the Catholic cemetery. Let them *dare* not bury you there." Then her face flushed deep red. "But you will want to be next to Selena."

"No. I want to be with you." He smiled so lovingly, and then so mischievously, she saw traces of his youthful dimples reappear. "What about... Why don't we get cremated?"

She brightened. "That would be perfect!"

"Who will get our ashes? Who would want them?"

"The River! Captain Wright can scatter them on the river from the ferry. He's a special friend of mine. He would do it."

"Done!"

"I will ask him to pick a moonlight night."

Once they had decided how they would dispose of their bodies, they felt relieved.

Father Passy wrote back that he would be there early on the date that she requested. He would be happy to give U.U. some informal, abbreviated instruction and perform the ceremony. They must get their license and take their blood tests ahead of time, of course.

Those inhabitants of Golden Gardens who are still sentient beings denounce, condemn, and castigate to the limits of their strength. The couple go through the blood tests, they get the marriage license. It is physically exhausting for both of them, but they are required to be there in person. After this day is over, they are tremendously relieved, the path is cleared. It is as if they have cut off the last grasping tentacles of a now-alien society. U.U. kisses Vanessa tentatively, then firmly, in her room when they get back at 4 P.M. She falls into bed, sleeps through her supper. The aide brings it on a tray, sets it within reach. Another aide comes in and removes the tray at nine o'clock. Mouche comes on at eleven, straight out of a three-way fight with her drunk husband and her gay son. She checks charts with a fragment of her mind, skips Vanessa's, she would check her later. It was galling to have to tend to that woman. Most of the staff wouldn't spit on her now.

Even had she read it, the chart would not have revealed to her that a shuffled 100-unit ampul of insulin had mistakenly been injected at 5 P.M. instead of the 40 units per millilitre that was her proper dosage.

Out on the river, moon tracks shine like the silver scales of all past fishdom floating on the water. Moonlight lies heaped over the earth white as fresh-grated cocoanut. Golden Gardens, Inc. is soaking in a milkbath that makes even it and its slatternly outbuildings look lovely and pure. And eerie.

A muggy, unsleepable Saturday night, and Gumbo is on the prowl. "Nah, nah, nah," he croons to a moaning child. "Nah, nah, nah-nah-nah, nah. Go to sleep, bébé." The child hushes until he leaves the room.

He hobbles down the hall and out of the juvenile unit. He checks on his mother-in-law. She is snoring and snorting desperately. A monster movie comes into Gumbo's head. "The sleep of the undead," he mutters. "It's a wonder she don't wake herself up." He continues his rounds, stops at Vanessa Derbigny's door. Since he has been shut out from the glow of the shining Nessa Derbigny his eyes have ceased to reflect light. They no longer anticipate something about to happen, good or bad.

He has not spoken to her since she has been in thick with U.U. Lumière. That she is living and moving and having her being outside of him, centered outside of him, is intolerable. And now they say she is going to marry U.U. Bitter hospital coffee and the undigested bolus of the contents of a bag of Paw-Paw's Cajun Spiced Pork Skins are playing leapfrog in his burning esophagus. He pushes open her door. He wants a face-down with her over this nigger. She can't do this to them, all of them in here. Golden Gardens is hell, yeah—but it is up to the ones in here who still have enough of a brain left, to keep it a respectable hell. Getting married to a nigger. *Married.* If it happens—if she marries a black man, then the whole world is a insane asylum.

She is sleeping heavily. There is a very sweet smile on her face, of peace, unlike the sweet, sad, always quizzical little smiles of the others here, the smiles that ask, "What's it all been about?" Her smile is saying, "Here is fullness at last." Gumbo experiences a surge of primitive jealousy as U.U.'s African face springs up zebra-striped in scarlet and ochre war paint from behind Vanessa's bed, not a man's face but the face of a wild animal, the dateless enemy from all times past, blackness itself.

"Miss Nessa! How you feel, chère? Miss Nessa!" No response. Her breath is deep and sighing. It smells like new-mown hay. He nudges her gently and then shakes and shakes her. "Oh, Miss Nessa, Dawlin'. Listen to me, wake up! Wake up!" Taking one hand from the crucifix that she holds on her breast, he feels a very fast but feeble pulse. She looks weak and her hands are cold. It could be insulin shock. His hand flashes to the call button next to her pillow, safely anchored by its lifeline around the bars of her bed, but he doesn't push the button. He pulls back, snatches open the little drawer in her bedside table. The hard candies, gaily wrapped, lay ready-to-hand. He must mash the button, quick, and insert one of those candies under her tongue. Messages are striking at his skull, as from swift crossed swords. What! What! He is paralyzed by a striking thought. Yes, God is taking care of this situation. God is in charge. "Gawd,

thank you, Gawd. Thank you, Gawd, in your infinite wisdom."
Vanessa moans, stirs, and whips her body side to side in the bed.
Gumbo's sinews jerk, his heart pounds, yet he stands transfixed,
hanging over the bed on his crutches. He can't stand to watch
her like this and not do anything. He gets the hell out of there,
sobbing.

The dead hand of 4 A.M. in a dead world. No one is around to
see his despair. He circumvents the nurses' station. Eventually
he gets hold of himself, gets back to the lobby somehow, draws
himself a shaky cup of coffee and lights a cigarette. In the smoke
he sees his wife's agitated, accusing face. "Now you show up," he
mutters. "Go back where you come from. What I done, I done."
He slumps at the table, alone in the big room. At the nurses'
station Mouche lights up, too, her mouth clamps down on the
cigarette and the bottom half of her face shifts sideways to
accommodate the match. After her illegitimate smoke, she
sprays a chemical into the air to drive away the smell, clips her
nails, files them, throws the nail file into a drawer under the
counter, curses her life, nods, sleeps.

At 4:45 A.M., just before the scheduled insulin injection, an
aide punches a call button and rushes from the room into the
hall to yell for help. The yell sets off Gumbo's mother-in-law,
who screams and screams. Mouche and the help find Vanessa,
dead scarcely half an hour, wadded at the end of her bed like the
pack off someone's back, having slid or thrashed her way down
there. The corpus of her crucifix is thrust face forward in the
pool of urine in which she also lies.

Outside, night still has the upper hand over the light of day.
Whitewashed to ghosts, the dogs of the town continue to bay,
not comprehending that the mystery is gone from the moon.